ARGUS STEPS IN

ARGUS STEPS IN

By Daniel Sernine

Translated by
Ray Chamberlain

Black Moss Press

© 1990 this translation Ray Chamberlain

Published by Black Moss Press
1939 Alsace St., Windsor, Ontario
N8W 1M5.

Black Moss Books are distributed in Canada
and the United States by Firefly Books, Ltd.,
250 Sparks Avenue,
Willowdale, Ontario, M2H 2S4.

Financial assistance toward publication of this book
was gratefully
received from the Canada Council and the
Ontario Arts Council.

COVER DESIGN BY BLAIR KERRIGAN/GLYPHICS
COVER ILLUSTRATION BY AMANDA DUFFY

Typesetting and page design by Kristina Russelo

Printed and bound in Canada.

Canadian Cataloguing in Publication Data
Sernine, Daniel
(Argus intervient. English)
Argus Steps In
(Young readers' library)
Translation of: Argus intervient.
ISBN 0-88753-216-0
I. Title. II. Title: Argus intervient. English. III. Series.
PS8587.E77A7413 1990   jC843'.54   C90-090408-9
PZ7.S37Ar   1990

Chapter One
Uranus's Blue Moon

Marc shuddered as the alarm rang out in the cockpit.

AUTOMATIC PILOT MALFUNCTION

said the monitor, urgently flashing on and off. The manual pilot gear sprang into view, as did the pedals for the antigrav system.

Through the narrow bay window in the front of the cabin, all that could be seen was a star-filled sky and a portion of the enormous globe of Uranus. But Marc was supposed to be landing on the planet's satellite Umbriel, not on the planet itself. The shuttle had its belly to the moon, and Marc could only see the surface in the form of a holograph. It was all ice, and seemed to glow with its own phosphorescence instead of with light reflected from Uranus. The surface was all peaks and crevices, midnight blue in the shadows and bluish white on the flat areas.

On the screen of the viseptor, the guide signal was dead. The base was displayed on the computer screen, and the landing area was underlined in white, but the radio-beacon wasn't working.

"The automatic pilot is supposed to be failsafe!" Marc protested between clenched teeth.

But no one answered him — the responsibility for the little ship was his alone. Marc changed the projection angle of the holograph. He could now see the base right in front of him: dark forms with rounded angles surrounded by a constellation of lights. The young man could distinguish the delicate green under several of the transparent domes; they looked awfully fragile.

An indicator light blinked on the control panel; there had been a sudden variation in the field of gravity. The moon was a tiny one and the planet was enormous; gravity on Umbriel was unstable.

"Just what I needed!" muttered the young pilot as he compensated for the shift.

He had to cut the antigrav if he wanted to continue his descent, or else he would overshoot the base without losing any further altitude.

He looked back at his monitor. Now his approach speed was too slow. His shuttle was heading for an ice-field just in front of the landing area. Using the throttle on his right, Marc fired the thrusters briefly.

At that moment the gravity came back, more abruptly than it had disappeared. The shuttle's descent accelerated into a dive.

"Oh no!"

His heart beating, Marc jammed down the antigrav pedal, but it was too late; the system had a longer reaction time than a classic thruster. In the holographic projection, he saw the buildings on the base rapidly grow larger; he saw through the transparent domes to the parks where the moon's residents were out walking.

With the throttle on his left, Marc put the retrothrusters on full power, and with the left pedal turned on the altivers. The jets whipped up a whirlwind of sparkling snow which hid the base. Now the numbers on his monitor were his only landmark, and Marc realised it was too late. He had avoided crashing and had regained altitude, but it wasn't quite enough. The shuttle hurtled into a parabolic antenna, tore it off and threw it against the nearest dome. The transplastal cracked, the air burst out like a hurricane, a gush of leaves and plants that blew away the whirling snow.

The impact had destroyed his retrothrusters and two of his altivers, and the shuttle plunged back to the ground. The angle was such that Marc could see through the bay window at the front of the cabin. There was just time to see the second dome, the one covering the agricultural area. The transplastal shattered on contact with his ship. The decompression was explosive: the shuttle, along with bushes and vegetables, robots and people, flew up in the tornado of escaping air.

For these unfortunate residents of Umbriel, death would have come quickly. But not so quickly that they wouldn't have known their fate: they would have felt themselves sucked up, lifted off the ground, suffocated and frozen all at the same time, before falling slowly down, hundreds of meters away, stiff and brittle as icicles, amid all the other debris from the disaster.

The double crash must have cracked the shuttle's cabin; the air was escaping with a sinister sounding hiss, and Marc could feel an icy stream of air. He hadn't had the time to slip into his space suit; now, there wouldn't be enough time to do so. On the control panel, everything blinked out...

Marc got up, went to the back of the shuttle and stepped out, a little shaken.

"Nice mess," said his flying instructor.

The boy wasn't proud of himself; he knew he should have banked the shuttle while it was regaining altitude, and gone back sooner to his altivers. He didn't have enough skill yet to make such a complicated manoeuvrer.

In the large simulation room, the instructor and her assistant were at their console. Seen from the outside, the flight simulator looked very little like a shuttle. In front of the cockpit's bay window, there was a large black space where the holograph was now back to normal: the blue surface of the planet, the base set in the ice, intact with its antennas and domes. On a giant screen, in the back, there were the blue-green globe of Uranus and the shining stars.

Marc protested, but without much conviction.

"You told me the automatic pilot never malfunctioned!"

"Theoretically, no. But we've got to be ready for everything; that's why we prefer to have human pilots on board. And I'm sorry to say that I don't think you're ready just yet."

She said this as gently as possible. But it was hard for Marc to accept. At his age, others were already co-pilots, while he was still having accidents in the flight simulator. The reason was that the others were boys and girls from Erymede, while Marc had only arrived from Earth three years ago. He had been fifteen years old, and was a video game champion as far as flying spacecrafts was concerned. But this was no longer a video game, and Marc was behind everyone else. He was doing fairly well in his courses, but in the practical and technical exercises, he was as handicapped as would be a boy from the twenties suddenly finding himself transplanted into 1990.

His instructor handed him his multifunction bracelet. "There was a call for you while you were in the simulator."

Marc pressed the tiny "calls-memory"

button. "Please be at Argus offices in Elysee at 9:00 p.m.," said a recorded voice.

Argus? the young man wondered as he put his multifunction bracelet back on. *What in the world can they want with me?*

Chapter Two
Some Mysteries on Arrival

Francis couldn't get over it. First, the chauffeured limousine waiting for them at Inverness airport. Then, after only a half-hour drive, the castle on the cliff. At a distance it didn't look like much, at the edge of the promontory. But close-up you could see exactly how big it was; and it was a veritable fortress.

The day was cool and misty, typical for coastal regions where the sea is cold. This was the Firth* of Moray, which empties into the North Sea. The country was Scotland, with its rugged and rarely sunlit landscape.

For Francis, everything seemed strange. He had never seen anything like this in Quebec, except perhaps on the North Shore. For Cynthia, the scene was a familiar one: she had been born in Edinburgh, and always spent the summer at the castle with her grandfather. This continued even after her family had moved to Montreal, where her father was the British Consul. This year, her eighteenth, she had brought the friend to whom she had so often spoken of her ancestral home.

The landscape was alternately covered with heather and small groves of trees. The road ran along a little river which flowed down from the Highlands. The river made its way into a gorge in the promontory*, which seemed to have been split by a giant's sword.

They came to a fork, and the limousine left the paved road for a dirt track which climbed up the promontory, in a series of hairpin turns.

Cynthia didn't understand her grandfather's attitude. First, he seemed not to want her at the castle this summer, though he was always overjoyed to have her visit him two months each year. The teenager couldn't figure out why this year he seemed so reticent. She had insisted so strongly that in the end he had given in: he had never been able to deny her anything.

"And then, when I phoned him yesterday, he said he had a surprise for me; that he was going to spoil me. I wonder what it is?"

"A new horse?" suggested Francis, a little ironically.

"He said that I was now a young woman. What do you get for a girl who has just become a young woman?"

"A husband?"

She squeezed his wrist with her thumb and her index finger, just between the two bones, until he cried out in pain.

But it was something else which took Francis's breath away. The road was now at the

12

edge of a precipice, the canyon which split the promontory in two. At its most narrow point, at the western end, a stone bridge spanned the canyon. The road across was narrow and dizzying; Francis barely dared to look down through the car window. He had a brief glimpse of the black cliffs and water foaming among the boulders, right at the bottom. Cynthia laughed at his fears.

The car passed through the barbacan, with the portcullis* and double doors opening automatically. A barbacan is a small watch tower built quite a ways in front of a fortress, as a first system of defence. Behind the thick walls and towers of the barbacan, there was a small house which had been built much more recently.

The road ran along the side of the cliff, with the void on one side, and a steep, sheer slope on the other which ended in a low wall. At the end of the road, the fortress displayed its slotted bastions, its stout towers, its massive dungeon and high watch tower. And also a forest of chimneys; strangely, these are what struck Francis the most. His girlfriend had once told him how many rooms there were; it would cost entire forests of wood to heat the entire castle. But Trevor MacKinnon lived there alone, and only occupied one of the corner towers, and part of the living quarters.

Finally the road came right up to the castle, a building much too vast to take in with a single glance.

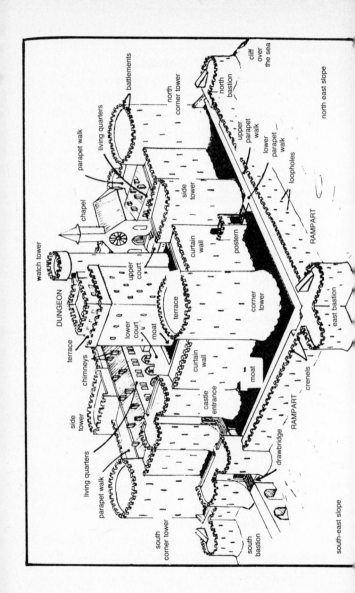

watch tower

battlements

north corner tower

cliff over the sea

parapet walk

living quarters

north bastion

chapel

side tower

north

upper parapet walk

curtain wall

postern

lower parapet walk

north east slope

loopholes

DUNGEON

upper court

RAMPART

terrace

lower court

terrace

corner tower

chimneys

moat

side tower

curtain wall

east bastion

living quarters

castle entrance

moat

crenels

parapet walk

RAMPART

drawbridge

south corner tower

south bastion

south-east slope

14

* * *

Francis couldn't get over (still couldn't!) the number of doors and portcullises they had to go through to get to grandfather MacKinnon.

He and his friend were now alone. Cynthia had started to run as soon as she got out of the car: she had hours of stiffness to shake off. She yelled out to the chauffeur that she knew the way, and she left him there with the luggage. Francis followed her, but didn't go so fast because there was so much to see.

Finally, they reached what Cynthia called the living quarters, a square surrounding the interior court of the castle. Near a corner in a corridor with a vaulting ceiling, Cynthia pointed to a door which opened onto a spiral staircase.

"If he's in the living room," she whispered, "we'll be able to surprise him. This isn't the door visitors normally come through."

In almost complete darkness, they silently climbed the stone steps which had been worn down by centuries of use. They stopped on a landing in front of a very old wooden door. Seeming puzzled, Cynthia put a warning finger up to her lips. Two men were talking and their voices were quite loud. Francis had some trouble understanding them because of their British accents.

"You seem to be forgetting that this is my home. This castle belongs to me; it's not a present someone gave me."

"You shouldn't have taken this assignment if you weren't ready to accept any compromises."

"I wasn't really given much choice."

"But you did take it on. Now you have to comply with security regulations."

"I've already complied with them more than I wanted to. But you not going to stop me receiving members of my own family!"

"The importance of this..."

"I know its importance, Dunfries, and I assure you that all proper security precautions will be taken. Now, leave; this discussion is just going round in circles!"

Cynthia took her friend's arm, and went back down the stairs to the corridor. They heard a door open and the voices were now calmer.

"This thing can't go on forever," said the man who had been voicing the objections. "The Service will put the pressure on soon."

"I certainly don't expect you to use any such tactics in this house."

"We'll talk again."

Cynthia and Francis, who had retraced their steps a little, now turned around as though they had just arrived. They saw a military man, a high ranking one, leave the living room by the main door. Another man, clad in a marine blazer, stayed at the door.

"Hello, grandfather."

"Cynthia!" cried the man in the blazer.

He hurried towards his granddaughter

without further thought of the officer, who turned his head as he walked off to give the teenagers a hostile look.

After having kissed MacKinnon, Cynthia made the introductions. MacKinnon, who was also in the military — a general in retirement — seemed less old than Francis had imagined him. He was at most sixty years old, and very well preserved. Only his hair, which was almost completely white, betrayed his age.

He invited Cynthia and Francis into his tower. It was a huge circular room with high narrow windows and no curtains. It served both as living and dining room, with luxurious furniture and a magnificent chimney.

There was another man there, a soldier whom MacKinnon presented as his aide-de-camp — his secretary, he said. He gave him leave, so he could be alone with his granddaughter and Francis. Again he hugged her, lengthily, and there was no doubt as to his sincerity and his joy. He had only had one son, whose career prevented him from seeing often; now that he was retired, he treated Cynthia as his own daughter. The summer was for him the happiest season of the year.

Cynthia wondered again why only a week ago he was so hesitant to welcome them.

After about an hour's conversation, MacKinnon started filling them in on what their holiday at the castle would be like.

"That surprise I was telling you about,"

he said to Cynthia with a sly smile. "You're are now almost a woman; and I know how young people are these days."

When they say that, thought Francis, *they're even more doddering than the average parent.*

"I thought you would prefer to spend your holidays in a little home of your own, without always running into old Trevor. I'm giving you the little house by the bridge; I had it redecorated for you. You'll feel at home; the chauffeur lives in a tower in the barbacan and won't disturb you. The cleaning will be done by my employees, and you won't have anything to do except cooking your meals, when you feel like it."

Cynthia didn't respond for a moment or two. She was more disappointed than happy: she and Francis could have been alone in any of the corner towers: the castle was so huge. In other years, her bedroom had been at the top of the north tower, and she had never complained about "old Trevor."

MacKinnon guessed at her disappointment.

"Of course," he said, "you can come and join me at mealtime whenever you wish."

"And can we go all over the castle? That's why Francis came."

"The castle, yes. Except for..."

"Except what?"

"Except for the dungeon. There were

some cracks discovered in the foundation, and I've had some engineers come to take a look. It's not safe to venture there until the repairs have been done."

The general wasn't telling the truth; Cynthia was convinced of that. The unusual sleeping arrangements, as well as the conversation they had overheard earlier, made her suspect that her grandfather was hiding something — reluctantly, perhaps. But she would find out what it was.

And right away she thought that in order to investigate, she had to lull any suspicions to sleep. She pretended to accept the arrangement her grandfather proposed with joy, and she promised to not to pester him about the dungeon — at least for now.

Chapter Three
Erymede's Defences

From Corinth, where the Admiralty and the Astronautical School were located, Marc took the inter-city to Elysee, after his unfortunate experience in the simulator. The inter-city ran between all the crater-cities on Erymede through a network of tunnels.

The young man wondered what Argus Organisation could possibly want with him. He hadn't had much to do with them since he had left Earth in rather dramatic circumstances*. He felt so depressed by his failure in the flight simulator that he wondered whether maybe they had decided to send him back to Earth, because he was to incompetent to succeed in whatever he was doing on Erymede. The very idea of being sent back there made him weak at the knees. What would happen to him? Was he still wanted by the R.C.M.P. and the Canadian army, from which he had barely escaped?

They'd never do that to me! They couldn't do that!

---

* See *Those Who Watch Over the Earth*.

20

The light suddenly brightened, and he was drawn from his grim reflections: the inter-city had just arrived at Elysee station. The train, which had slowed without his even noticing, stopped softly.

Marc got off the train. Through Elysee station's immense glass walls could be seen the city park.

Another inter-city, with its streamlined hull and tinted windows, came to a halt across the platform.

"Marc!"

The boy turned his head; one of the passengers was calling him. He recognised his friend Carl, the one who had saved his life by bringing him to Erymede. They shook hands. Carl asked him what brought him to the capital.

Marc told him about the intriguing summons.

"That's strange," said Carl. "I received the same summons, and for the same time."

On their way, they discussed what such a summons could possibly mean.

"I heard," said Carl, "that it had something to do with an Earth mission."

They were walking along the many escalators and foot-bridges that led from the station. There was something Carl wanted to see before going to the Argus offices:

"We'll have time. It happens around 20:00."

"What's that?"

"You don't read the information bulletins? The defence system has to be activated tonight."

Erymede, which was part of the asteroid belt between Mars and Jupiter, had been accelerated to accomplish its orbit in 365 and a quarter days, like Earth. This meant that Erymede moved much more quickly that the other asteroids, which then seemed to be moving towards it. Sometimes, one of them was directly in the way of Erymede's trajectory, and it became necessary to pulverise it.

"Let's go to the outside gallery; we'll be able to see well from there."

This gallery, on the periphery of the crater, had a panoramic view through its floor-to-ceiling windows.

"We're here just in time," said Carl.

On the plain (which was in fact too uneven to be called a "plain"), three-sided, pyramid-shaped structures were beginning to open. At the same time, the platforms under them were rotating like an observatory dome. But instead of telescopes, there were formidable laser-cannons starting to appear.

The asteroid endangering Erymede wasn't yet visible to the naked eye, of course. But you could tell where it was from the direction the cannons were aiming. And Marc thought he saw a bright speck moving slowly, getting bigger as he watched it.

The guns began to fire. Double beams appeared, lines of energy between Erymede and space. They were barely visible, just thin, light blue lines, not dazzling at all — except for anything in their path!

All this happened in total silence, of course, but you could feel the entire might of Erymede behind these beams, all the power of the nuclear fusion reactors buried in the heart of the planetoid.

In the inky sky, the pale, tiny speck was suddenly a bright pink, spewing little glowing sparks which, in reality, must have been enormous chunks of molten rock. Then, there was the explosion, still in total silence: it looked like a white sun shot through with fleeting tinges of blue, green and yellow. The tiny sun burned out, leaving nothing but a cloud of ionised gas, which glimmered for several seconds, a lingering trace.

The lasers stopped, and the parabolic antennas wavered slightly on the gun-carriages, following the path of the debris from the asteroid, making sure that none of it threatened to strike Erymede.

But there was no danger of that: the cannons were rehoused, the pyramids closed. It was over. For Erymede, it was an event of such little importance that few citizens had even bothered to watch. But Marc shivered, thinking of what would befall a spacecraft which would dare to attack Erymede — if Earthlings ever came to build warships.

Chapter Four
Someone in the Dungeon

General MacKinnon invited Cynthia and her boyfriend to dinner in the west tower. The table on the first floor, at which he had received them that afternoon, could easily seat eight; the three place-settings at one end appeared lost. With the meal finished, MacKinnon and his guests rose from the table to sip their coffee in more comfortable chairs.

Before sitting down, Francis went to a window to see the view from this corner of the castle. The afterglow from the setting sun was still visible in the west as was the pale foam, slapping up against the shore. Beyond the other shore of the estuary were the rounded crests of the Northern Highlands.

"Is it true that you can see the famous Loch Ness from here?" asked Francis.

"From the top of the watchtower, yes, on a clear day. But you know, it's nothing to see."

"Have you ever seen the Monster?"

"Never," answered MacKinnon, laughing. But Francis didn't laugh. He leaned over the open window and noticed an almost vertical drop from the castle wall to the cliff below, where the waves crashed and roared against the reef. Francis withdrew, closed the window and returned to the security of the living room.

The General asked Cynthia to light the fire which had been prepared in the hearth. All three sat before it watching the rising flames. "It's story-time," said Cynthia with a wry smile.

"Come now, you know them all by heart!"

"But Francis hasn't heard them all. Tell us why there's a curse on the castle."

"It's cursed?" interrupted Francis skeptically.

"Oh yes," replied the grandfather. So without further coaxing, he told them how, toward the end of the fifteenth century, a traveller from Europe had visited the castle. He was from Eastern Europe, perhaps the Carpathian Mountains, or Transylvania maybe. He was cordially received by the castle lord, but during a banquet, he was slighted by one of the MacKinnon sons, and lost an eye in the duel that followed. In the room where they carried him, his face bathed in blood, he vowed to avenge his disfigurement. It was believed that his words were those of a man gone mad with pain, but during the night, his room was the scene of alarming phenomena: bizarre lights in the windows, incense fumes filtering through under the door, the sound of mighty voices — not the traveller's — and distant music or chanting which seemed to come from everywhere at once. At dawn, the lord of the castle, accompanied by an armed escort, knocked on his door, and ordered him to put an end to the sorcery and leave the castle at once. A long silence followed, which permeated the whole fortress. Everyone was alarmed, sensing that something terrible was about to happen. Suddenly, there was a blinding flash; the air itself, throughout the whole castle, seemed to blaze; the inner courtyard, the covered archways, the hallways and towers, right down into the cellars where there were no windows. A deafening shriek shook the citadel, hundreds of screeches, filled with pain and suffering; every courtier, every servant, every guard, every member of the MacKinnon family was blinded, and their hands and faces slightly scorched. Panic filled the place; some broke their necks on the stone staircases, others were injured running blindly, driven wild. Then, over the lamenting of all these people, was heard the loud voice of the visitor. He had climbed onto the terrace at the top of the dungeon and uttered his curse. Now blind in one eye, he was blinding others. But his vengeance did not stop there; impossible to defend against, it would endure for ten generations in every imaginable form. The castle lord ordered that the sorcerer be captured. But his blinded soldiers were helpless against this one-eyed wizard who amused himself by knocking them down the stairs, pushing them through the crenels*, drowning them in the castle moat. There was great confusion. When calm was restored, the stranger had left with his horses and valet.

Cynthia nodded and smiled. Old Trevor had not lost his gifts as a storyteller. If she were still eight and not eighteen, she'd still have goosebumps and be glancing suspiciously toward the windows. Francis, for his part, was unable to take the account as anything but a story. "Did your family suffer other misfortunes?" he asked. Without taking offence at his irony, MacKinnon said yes. But at that very moment, there was a knock at the door. It was McSweeny, the secretary. He entered without being asked, which seemed to irk the General. The lieutenant was still in uniform. He appeared very sure of himself and Francis disliked him intensely, being unaccustomed to military decorum.

"We've had a call from General Dunfries," announced the man, walking toward his superior.

"He never gives me a moment's rest. What does he want now?"

MacKinnon's secretary bent over and whispered a few words in his ear. Immediately, the General looked grim, even troubled. While it didn't go unnoticed with Cynthia, she didn't let on. If she was to be free to pursue her inquiry, she must appear unaware. "I'll have to finish the story some other time, children," said MacKinnon getting up from his chair. The youngsters bade him goodnight, and left the same way they came in, arriving in the upper courtyard. A few lanterns shone, ancient lamps where electricity had replaced candles. In the middle of the inner courtyard stood the dungeon, massive and square, with the watchtower in one of the corners.

The upper floors were lost in darkness; a shadow was all that could be distinguished against the starlit sky. Cynthia thought she noticed a glow coming from above, and some movement. "Look!" she murmured.

"What?"

"On the top floor of the dungeon. A light."

"I don't see anything."

"It didn't last long." They lingered for a moment, faces turned upwards, and then

Francis made a move to go. "There's nothing. Let's go." She followed him against her will. They went down into the lower courtyard and through the archway that led out of the castle. As she was about to leave, Cynthia turned and looked again toward the dungeon, and the terrace surrounding the last floor. "There's someone there," she whispered. Francis looked too, but he could scarcely make out the parapet. "The last crenel on the left," uttered Cynthia.

"There's no..."

Nobody? What about this silhouette, this shape, this slightly lighter spot, could it not be a torso or a face? The light thrown by the courtyard lanterns didn't reach that high so it was impossible to say whether someone was there or that it was an illusion. "Let's go," suggested Francis, in a soft voice. "Your grandfather has us imagining things, with his ghost stories."

Indeed, it was from up there that the Transylvanian traveller, according to Trevor, had cursed the castle.

Chapter Five
The Argus Meeting

The Argus offices on Erymede, like all the Elysee's administrative departments, faced an atrium, a sort of inner courtyard enclosed with glass walls, decorated with luxurious plants and fountains.

In a conference room, Marc and Carl were introduced to someone from Argus Operations. Lea Laredo seemed to be sitting in front of them, on the other side of the table, whereas she was in fact on the Moon, nine million kilometres away. It was her holographic image which was projected on Erymede, just as theirs was projected on Argus. Thanks to tachyons, which had recently replaced lasers, the transmission was practically instantaneous.

Marc, who had been on Erymede for three years, was still not used to speaking to a shimmering, translucent image as though it was a real person. Carl was much more at ease; he seemed to know Lea Laredo quite well.

Although nervous at first, Marc became gradually more relaxed. His recent fears appeared unjustified; no one was reprimanding him for his failures at the Astronautical School.

Lea Laredo began her briefing.

"Let me introduce you to Grigor Syeline, a Soviet physician."

On the small screens sunk into the conference table there appeared a photograph of a man in his late thirties or perhaps early forties.

"Until recently, he was working in the neurological institute at Tallinn, where he was leading the research into epilepsy and brain-waves."

Hearing this, Marc and Carl exchanged glances.

"I know that this area is not unknown to Marc Alix," she said.

In fact, he was very familiar with it; his uncle Horace Guillon worked in the field, and Marc had served for some time as his assistant. The affair had had a tragic ending for the doctor; he stood up against the army and the police, who wanted to use his discoveries for military purposes.

"Like Dr. Guillon in America, professor Syeline, three years later, discovered that it's possible to regularise the electric currents in the brain, currents whose disruption causes epilepsy. But his research took a different direction from that of Guillon, and he found, at least in theory, that waves emitted at a certain frequency can totally paralyse all brain activity, although only temporarily and without causing death.

"As soon as he realised how the military could make use of this discovery, he interrupted his research and resolved to escape from the Soviet Union. This occurred just before a worldwide conference on neurology in Norway. In Oslo, he talked about his plan to escape with a British colleague, whom he considered a trusted friend. Unfortunately, this man, Wesley, was a consultant for NATO and he relayed this information to the military.

"With the greatest of secrecy, Wesley offered Syeline the means to defect to the West. Syeline had no family in the Soviet Union, and few friends; only one thing held him back, the fear that his son would be kidnapped. Syeline's wife was Finnish, and she had returned with the boy to live in Helsinki several years ago. She died last year, but Niki continued to study in Helsinki, staying with an aunt.

"Wesley promised that someone would fetch the boy; friends, members of Amnesty International, he said, would take care of it. Syeline therefore decided to prolong his stay in Oslo. The Soviets began to suspect him, especially since an assistant to the professor arrived at the same hypothesis as Syeline about the paralysis frequency. The government ordered Syeline to return so that he could begin work on this potential weapon. The K.G.B. tried to bring him back by force, but agents from NATO got to him just in time. The same day, NATO agents got hold of his son Niki in Helsinki, right under the noses of the Soviets. Syeline talked to him by phone when Niki was in Stockholm; he was doing well and was being treated very considerately, and was promised that he would soon be taken to his father.

Marc listened carefully to this story. It was very similar to that of his uncle and himself. Horace Guillon had refused to allow his research to be used by the military. He died as a result, and Marc was almost killed too, trying to escape government agents.

"All this," continued Lea Laredo, "happened this week. It was all kept very quiet, of course, but nothing escapes the attention of Argus. Well, almost nothing; we don't know for the moment where Syeline was taken. We know he's in one of the NATO countries, and we're almost certain it's the United Kingdom. We'll have more precise intelligence on that tomorrow."

"And our mission?" asked Carl. "I imagine you have some sort of mission in mind for us?"

It wasn't hard for him to guess; at the time he had met Marc, he was working in Recruitment, but now he was in Operations, and he regularly had missions in Great Britain and northern Europe.

"Listen. It was simple naïvete on Syeline's part to believe that the Western powers would not ask him to use his research discoveries to develop some form of weapon. He will

33

probably continue believing this until he realises that the people helping him aren't from
Amnesty International at all, but are NATO
agents instead. And that will happen some time;
the NATO military will voice their demands,
knowing that the Soviets will start developing a
weapon several months from now, using some
of Syeline's old colleagues. Argus's intention is
to rescue the doctor and his son, and to offer
them a new identity in the country of their
choice, safe from the great powers."

"Hold on," Marc interrupted, "What do I
have to do with any of this? I have no training
for..."

"First, let me tell you right away that you
are entirely free to either accept or refuse this
mission. But, look at this picture."

On their screens appeared a photograph
of a teenager, fifteen or sixteen years old, with
blue eyes and brown hair.

"Well! Look at that!" Carl exclaimed.

"What?" asked Marc.

"Don't you see? You two could be twins!"
Marc pouted.

"You think so?"

"If you just dyed your hair, you'd be his
double. Is this Niki Syeline?"

"That's right," said Lea Laredo.

Marc wasn't convinced.

"He's a lot younger than I am."

"But he's big for his age. He's almost your
height."

"And so what's the plan — you want me
to take his place?" He asked this casually, but as

he said it, he realised that might be it; maybe they wanted to send him back to Earth for good!

His anxiety must have shown, because Lea Laredo was quick to reassure him.

"Absolutely not. That would be much too risky; the agents who are guarding him are not amateurs. No, we're still not clear on how you will be involved. That will depend on what happens to the boy, and on how the father's attitude evolves. We would just like you to be available should we need you. You'd go to Earth with Carl Andersen, but there woud be other agents with him if things got messy."

Marc felt better; he knew the Erymeans well enough to know they would never stab him in the back. But he wasn't any the more drawn to the mission; if the truth were told, even though three years had passed, he was still wary of Earthlings after the threats and violence he had undergone at the hands of their military and police.

Lea Laredo detected his hesitation through his hologram on the moon.

"This is fairly urgent, Marc. Can't you at least come with Carl to Argus, and postpone your decision until then? In the meanwhile we'll have more information and a better idea of what role you could play."

The young man sighed, still hesitant.

"All right," he said, finally.

It might do him good to take a couple of days off from the Astronautical School, anyway.

Chapter Six
A Stranger in the Mist

In the morning, the hill and castle were shrouded in fog. The fresh air carried with it the scent of the sea.

Cynthia and Francis casually made their way up to the fortress. Rather than take the path that hugged the cliff, they chose the brushpath on the south-east slope of the cape. Though it was not steep, it was uneven and covered with clusters of heather. Francis had the impression that he was on a planet without a horizon, a strange land that came to an end a few metres before him. The only light source was a luminous patch of sky. The sun was hidden.

Little by little, a mass appeared before the youngsters: the castle emerging from the fog, or rather the rampart in front of the castle which was its first line of defense.

They came to the edge of the ditch which was on the near side of the rampart. Francis thought he could make out a human silhouette in one of the crenels of the tower closest to them. But when he took a closer look, he no longer saw anything.

The drawbridge was down and the port-cullis was raised. Only the massive double-doors were closed, but Cynthia had the key to the electric lock. Now the youngsters were on the other side of the battlement wall, but instead of continuing on toward the castle, they strolled along the inner parapet walk.

They stepped inside the rampart where there was a corridor lined with loopholes through which the enemy could be fired on.

These were dark and damp places, where every step echoed as through a cavern. The young visitors moved forward cautiously, giving their eyes time to adapt to the darkness. Here and there, a hint of daylight filtered through the loopholes at the far end of their narrow passageways to each of the loopholes. Everything was just as Cynthia had described it to Francis, and despite his seventeen years, he trotted along, enthusiastic. To think that this place was almost a thousand years old, and here we was walking aloft where soldiers clad in mail once patrolled.

"Did you hear that?" whispered Cynthia.

"What?"

"A noise, like a metal clang."

Could there be someone else inside the rampart? Last night, the old man MacKinnon, had said half-jokingly, that the castle was haunted. Even during the day?

Near the last guard room toward the end of the archway, a trestle with a sign blocked the

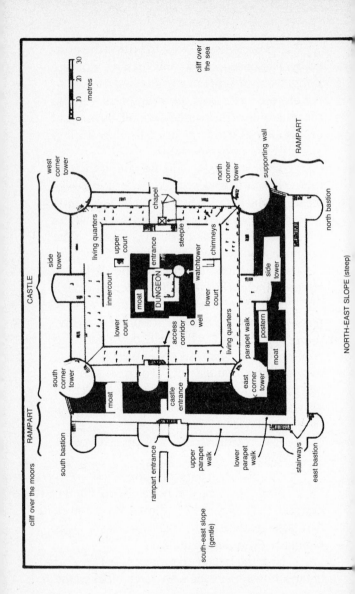

cliff over the sea

CASTLE

west corner tower

side tower

living quarters

upper court

chapel

entrance

inner court

DUNGEON

moat

steeple

watchtower

chimneys

north corner tower

supporting wall

RAMPART

north bastion

lower court

well

lower court

side tower

south corner tower

moat

access corridor

living quarters

parapet walk

postern

moat

RAMPART

castle entrance

east corner tower

south bastion

rampart entrance

upper parapet walk

lower parapet walk

stairways

east bastion

south-east slope (gentle)

cliff over the moors

NORTH-EAST SLOPE (steep)

metres
0 10 20 30

38

narrow passageways to each of the loopholes:
DANGER, it read.

"The moat water has weakened the wall
at this end of the ramparts," explained Cynthia.
"The sign was there last summer. But I thought
the whole bastion was off limits."

They went down a few steps and into a
triangular room where the vaulted ceiling was
supported by three pillars. On the back wall,
between two windows (real windows, not just
slits). was a large fireplace with its massive
chimney.

This time, it was Francis who thought he
heard something; the shuffling sound of shoes
on the spiral staircase that led to the bastion
terrace.

"Could there be someone else visiting
the rampart?" Francis asked his friend.

She moved closer to him.

"I wonder who. It's been a long time
since Grandfather explored his own castle, and
the hired help weren't interested either.
Maybe..."

A defening crashing noise interrupted
her. The youngsters turned around, instinc-
tively hunching their shoulders and covering
their heads with their arms to protect themselves. At the far end of the room, the stones
from the chimney came tumbling down, shattering noisily against the stone floor. A bitter
smoke soon filled the room.

"Quick, everything's going to fall!" cried
Cynthia grabbing her friend's arm.

Coughing from the smoke, they ran up the spiral staircase two steps at a time and sprang outdoors. The chimney, still intact, was sending out smoke which became thinner as it rose.

"Don't you think that's a lot of smoke for a simple cloud of dust?" observed Cynthia immediately. "Surely, that couldn't be pulverised brick?"

Francis nodded, a bit shaken.

"And look," added Cynthia, pointing to the moat water which was moving in concentric waves away from the bastion. "Something heavy has fallen into the water, maybe something was thrown. But the chimney is intact, it hasn't lost a brick."

"Something thrown by what?"

"What did you hear down there, before everything collapsed?"

Francis wasn't sure. A tremor, like the sound of a falling rock shattering against the ground. Or an explosion.

"That would explain the smoke," concluded Cynthia.

She inspected the ramparts and the upper and lower parapet* walks; as far as the fog allowed them to see there was no one in sight. If someone had fled after the explosion, Cynthia and Francis would have seen them. It was a long way to the next sheltered area. Unless he were hiding in a crenel or a loophole space.

Without a moment's hesitation, the girl

jumped down three metres to the lower parapet, landing with the grace of a gymnast.

"You check all the crenels from here to the double bastion. I'll look into the loopholes."

"Do you think that..."

"And be careful! This person wants to hurt us."

Francis set out. He was nervous. A ghost setting off an explosion? More likely a flesh and blood person. Had he tried to kill them?

But there was no one in the crenels, no one trying to hide by hanging outside the ramparts; to leap into the ditch was unthinkable: it was at least a 10-metre drop.

When he came to the double bastion which stood at the corner of the rampart, the teenager called off his search; if the person had made it this far, he would have had time to make a getaway by a number of different paths.

Somewhat hesitatingly, Francis hung from his arms, and let himself drop to the lower parapet. Cynthia came back toward the stone culvert which was connected to the castle by a little lift bridge beside one of the side-towers.

"The person could have had time to come into the castle through this door," Cynthia figured. "It seems to me that this drawbridge isn't usually down."

She walked along the footbridge and tried to open the postern*.

"Locked," she noted.

Francis cast a worried look toward the

41

crenels over the footbridge from which a stone could easily be dropped on his friend's head.

"What's going on, do you think?"

She didn't know, but she was determined to find out.

"Let's go back to the guard room."

The boy would have preferred not to, but he remained silent.

At the north bastion, they went back down. The smoke had dissipated but the acrid smell lingered. Bynthia would've loved to know what that smell was; she was almost sure that it was the smell of explosives.

She came over to the chimney, stepping over some of the stones that lay on the ground. It was ripped open from the mantle up, and the damper lying in the hearth was completely twisted. Yet it hadn't been crushed by falling rocks. Cynthia reached over and touched the metal plate; it was still warm. There had definitely been an explosion, and the chimney, already weak, had collapsed. The girl remembered that it had had cracks in it; that was why the room was off limits.

"It was premeditated," confirmed Cynthia, "the person moved the 'Danger' sign so that we'd come into the room."

"Let's go see your grandfather," suggested Francis, afraid that the vaulted ceiling might tumble down at any moment.

They climbed to the upper parapet. The fog was slowly disappearing, being burnt off by the warmth of the sun; giving a clearer view. From the inside, the large towers of the castle appeared within arm's reach.

As they walked along, Cynthia thought of the timeliness of alerting her grandfather. She wondered whether the incident wasn't somehow connected to the other mysteries surrounding the MacKinnon castle.

With its peak illuminated by the slanting rays of the sun, the dungeon seemed to float above the layer of fog that still concealed the lower floors. It looked like the prow of some tall ship made of stone. At the top of the double bastion, Cynthia turned around to gaze upon the dungeon, giving herself time to think.

"Look," she said suddenly, without raising her voice or making a move.

On the dungeon's terrace, the terrace that surrounded the last floor, there was someone. This time, there could be no doubt. A man, blond, young looking, in his late twenties maybe. Fair skin, rather long hair, and a beige sweater over his shirt. He was walking behind the crenels, slowly, as if he were out for a stroll. But he appeared pensive with his hands behind his back and a vacant look in his eyes.

"Do you think he's the one you saw last night?" asked Francis in a subdued voice.

"Maybe, but anyway the dungeon isn't closed off as grandfather led us to believe. I wonder why he lied."

At that moment, the man noticed them

from the top of the tower. The youngsters felt his eyes fixed on them. He stared at them, without moving.

"He looks sad, don't you find?" asked Cynthia, without taking her eyes off him.

Francis wasn't sure.

"It's simple," decided the young woman, "we'll go say hello."

They went down and crossed the moat. Here too the drawbridge was lowered and the portcullis raised. Only the first of the three doors was closed, and Cynthia had the key.

With Francis behind her, she crossed the lower courtyard, climbed to the upper courtyard from which one could get to the dungeon, the central tower of the castle. But, like yesterday, the little drawbridge was raised. Cynthia no longer understood. Had the man closed himself off in the dungeon? She couldn't believe he was there without her grandfather knowing it. Was he the one who just tried to blow up the bastion?

She looked toward the west tower where Trevor MacKinnon's bedroom was. Between the chimneys of the living quarters, she noticed one of the windows — her grandfather was standing there watching Cynthia and Francis; he looked concerned.

"Come on," said Cynthia, heading for the occupied wing. "Grandfather is motioning us to come up."

"Should we tell him about he explosion?"

"We'll see. Don't say anything."

They went in, one floor above where they had been received the night before. This level was of course circular also, but had been made into a library and drawing room; this was where the General's office was.

MacKinnon was there waiting; McSweeny too. He must have hurried to get there. Cynthia decided to forget about her stance of yesterday and address the question head on.

"There's someone at the top of the dungeon. Isn't he in danger if the dungeon could collapse at any time?"

MacKinnon smiled and nodded his head slightly.

"I was wrong to lie to you, you're too shrewd a girl. the truth is, the dungeon isn't any more cracked that my skull."

This admission seemed to anger McSweeny, who had trouble hiding his irritation.

"You see, I'd have preferred that you didn't come here this summer."

"What's wrong?"

"Oh, it's a family problem, a sad story."

Except for her grandfather, Cynthia knew little about he MacKinnon family. She had no uncles or aunts, and was under the impression that Trevor had only one sister.

"I agreed to help one of my cousins, a childhood friend. His son is...sick, disturbed, you might say. But my cousin doesn't want him interned; he loathes psychiatric asylums. Since my cousin can't keep him at home this summer, he asked me to look after him."

"He's crazy?"

"That's a cruel way of saying it. Let's just say that he doesn't always have his wits about him. His mind wanders and he can go for days without speaking. Other times, he seems to be delirious. He speaks calmly but tells incredible stories in which everyone is persecuting him. But most of the time, he's like you and me, perfectly lucid. He reads a lot, writes poems. He's gentle and harmless."

"Then, why lock him up?"

"He's not really 'locked up.' He has the whole dungeon to himself, and comes out on the terrace when he wishes. Occasionally, I take him out for walks in the country. But he needs supervision."

"Is he ever violent? Are you sure he can't leave the dungeon without you knowing it?"

"Oh no, he can't get out alone. But I've never seen him violent. Sometimes he runs away, disappearing for weeks on end, then returning thin and underfed. He once caused an accident crossing the road. He can't be left alone."

A sad story indeed, thought Cynthia. Why had she never heard tell of him? True enough, it was a situation that people didn't talk about willingly.

"Won't we be allowed to speak to him?" asked the girl.

"I'd rather not. For the time being at least. We'll see how he gets on."

Cynthia nodded pensively. A mad poet locked up in a tower, a handsome, blond poet with sad eyes. She would have liked to meet him. She would speak gently to him, and try to reach beyond his madness. Intuitively, she didn't believe that he was the man who had destroyed the chimney in the northern bastion. He would have had time if he'd used the castle's secret underground passageways; but if he knew about hem, then he wouldn't stay locked up in the dungeon.

"So," she concluded, "the dungeon is in no danger of caving in?"

"Not at all," replied Trevor, laughing.

"Because the northern bastion almost came down on our heads."

MacKinnon gasped in alarm. But Cynthia noticed that McSweeny remained impassive. *It would have pleased him,* she thought.

Chapter Seven
The NORDRI Survivor

There was mayhem at Corinth's astro-port when Marc and Carl arrived, the day after their briefing at the Argus offices. The crews of the patrol ships Sleipnir and Skoll had been recalled and were boarding shuttles to get back on board.

Marc recognised a friend, a trainee on board the Skoll; she was waiting her turn to get on the shuttle. He asked her what was going on.

"You didn't hear the news? The supply ship Nordri was caught in a hypenar forcefield somewhere around the Martian orbit."

"Was it destroyed?"

"There could be survivors."

She couldn't tell him anything else; the shuttle had docked and crewmembers were rushing to get on board.

Things were quieter now. Carl and Marc waited for their astrobus, whose departure had been delayed a little. Marc was thinking of what he knew about hypenars. They were one of the dangers of space travel, something about which not much was known. They seemed to come out of nowhere, suddenly appearing in any given place and then disappearing after an instant, just as suddenly. They were zones of pure energy, huge luminous clouds, hundreds of thousands of kilometres wide. Anything in its vicinity was destroyed, annihilated. All reactors functioning in its sphere of influence had abrupt power surges — and generally exploded. Hypenars and neguenars were the nightmare of space travellers, just as reefs and icebergs were the curse of sailors.

Carl and Marc found two seats together at the front of the bus. They turned on a screen to get the most recent news. nothing was known of the Nordri after its distress signal which had been sent by the survivors of the explosion; they had had to use all the rest of the ship's energy to send that transmission. Now, only the automatic distress signal, indicating the position of the wreck, was being received.

The huge sliding roof of the astroport opened, and the astrobus lifted gently off the ground and into the open air — or rather into open space, as there was no atmosphere on Erymede. Then the thrusters took over from the antigrav. Their jetstream made the surface of the asteroid shine with a pale glimmer. The bus rose diagonally, then banked in a large arc and set off towards the sun.

Marc was thinking. Space was so danger- ous; why did he want to become a pilot so much? He could stay on Erymede safely; there were lots of interesting things to do, particularly in the field of research. But the reason he had left Earth was so that he could get to know outer space. It wasn't so that he could closet himself in subterranean galleries and under the domes of Erymede.

It was strange that Marc was so awkward at flying a shuttle but so skilled in moving himself around in space; in his exercises with the spacesuit and the indivijet, he was at the top of his class. This was apparently because he had a very keen sense of balance and inertia.

The hours came and went. Even though Marc's heart wasn't in it, he and Carl chatted in English to practice in case the mission should take place in Great Britain. Marc was scheduled to receive the basics of Russian by hypno-education in case he had to meet Grigor Syeline. Hypno-education was a process by which instruction was given when the subject was half asleep, because the learner was so much more receptive then.

Through the transparent partition, they could see the cockpit, identical to that of a shuttle.

"Something's happening," said Marc.

In fact, both the pilot and copilot seemed excited. A blip had appeared on the repector screen, which was scanning space in the direction of the wreck of the Nordri, just in case. The anabservor was aimed at it, and the computer

50

determined the precise dimensions and composition of the object, as well as its path and point of origin. As soon as this information was in, the pilot redirected the astrobus. The voice of the copilot was then heard over the speaker system, addressing the passengers.

"We've located an object traveling out of the zone where the supply ship Nordri was destroyed. First indications are that it is a small ship. We're going to approach the craft to see if it is carrying passengers."

Marc couldn't resist opening the transparent door and putting his head in the cockpit. He knew the copilot, Vermasen, who had been a teacher at the Astronautical School.

"There's nothing but the automatic distress signal," she said. "The main antenna must have been broken."

The video screen showed the greatest possible enlargement of the object in question. It was one of the mini-tugs which was used to move containers in space.

"Do you think anyone is on board?" asked Marc.

"The question is, why would one of the survivors have left his companions and the wreck?"

"Unless," said the pilot, "this person was in the tug when the disaster happened. May the tug was torn away from the Nordri, incapable of returning or even of steering. Look; its thrusters are damaged."

"Only the verniers seem to be intact," said Vermasen. "That's what enabled them to stabilise the tug."

"We'll have to go out there to rescue the person," said Marc.

"That's exactly what I'll do," Vermasen replied, after looking at the pilot.

"I'm going with you," Marc decided.

"What?!" Carl, the pilot and the copilot all burst out at once.

"I can do it," the young man insisted. "I have my credits from the Astronautical school. In fact, those are the only ones I do have," he said in a lower tone of voice.

"Yes, I recognise you, Marc Alix," said Vermasen. "But even so, this isn't just an exercise."

"You can't do it alone. Do you think that anyone else among the passengers is qualified?"

The pilot asked this question over the speaker system. Nobody volunteered; the astrobus was only half full and it just so happened that not one of the passengers had any training in this field. Marc got his way.

"All right," said the copilot. "But don't play the hero; I'm in charge."

Followed by Carl, who was still vaguely protesting the whole thing, the two of them made their way to the rear hold, while the pilot tried to manoeuvre the astrobus in front of the tug and adjust his speed.

Rez Vermasen and Marc got into their

spacesuits equipped with indivijets, those mini-rockets attached to the forearms and calves that helped one to move in space. The voice of the pilot echoed in their helmets.

"The tug's hull is damaged; the cabin is probably depressurised. If there is any survivor, he has only a spacesuit's worth of air. And given the time since the disaster, that supply must almost be gone."

Vermasen and Marc hurried towards the small airlock between the main cabin and the exit. The air was pumped out, and they opened the hatch at the stern. There headlights were already on.

The wreck was there in front of them, about ten meters away, brilliantly lit. The stars were barely visible in the infinite blackness of space. Vermasen led, attaching herself to the hatchway to avoid floating adrift; she opened a small compartment in the hull of the vessel. She took out a pistol, which had a thin cord attached. She wedged her feet into the corners of the door and told Marc to hold on to her. He grabbed her shoulder, anchoring himself meanwhile by clutching a rung in the airlock.

She took aim at the tug. There was no sound, of course; just a small cloud of condensed gas spouting from the barrel. The cord unrolled behind the magnetic missile which stuck to the hull of the wreck. Vermasen threw the pistol behind her, into the airlock, and then operated the crank that was fitted into the hull of the astrobus. Slowly she reeled the wreck towards the astrobus, until it hit the metal framework deployed about three meters from the airlock and serving as a sort of bumper.

Once the threat of collision was out of the way, Marc left the chamber with a life pack. There was no light in the tug's cabin, and the tinted porthole made it impossible to see inside.

"There's someone in there with a spacesuit," said Marc, "but I don't know if he's alive."

Grabbing onto whatever he could, the young man made his way towards the hatchway of the tug, which was behind or below, depending on the tug's relative position. He had chosen the sunlit side, so that he could keep his back to the dazzling glare of the star. Vermasen arrived the same time he did.

"I hope the impact didn't damage the mechanism."

The automatic opening device wasn't working. All the electric energy available must have been used to augment the strength of the distress signal as much as possible. Vermasen fiddled with the manual device. After some effort, the hatch opened, its two panels moving apart.

Marc dove in, his frontal searchlight shining. The light reflected off the screens and control panels. There was someone sitting in the command seat, his helmet connected to the emergency supply of air in the cabin. The telltale light was red.

Marc was alarmed, but he didn't panic. He calmed and steadied himself, and already his hands were at work. He pulled out the tube from the life pack and skillfully connected it to the person's helmet. Only after he got the green light signalling that all was well did he disconnect the tube from the empty emergency supply.

Was he too late? If the red light had only been on a couple of minutes, there was some chance the person might recover. Any longer, and he was either dead or his brain was irreparably damaged.

"Is he moving?" asked Vermasen from behind.

"Not yet. I'm giving him air."

Marc started to undo the straps that held the body to the seat. Then he moved so he could attach the life pack to the back of the spacesuit. Only then did he attempt to manoeuvre himself in the narrow cabin so that he could get the body out of the tug.

"Can you help me back up?" he asked Rez.

From outside, she grabbed him by the ankles and pulled him gently towards herself. There's nothing easier, in a weightless state; the principal problem is one of inertia and bulk.

Without too much difficulty they transferred the body to the airlock of the astrobus. They closed the hatch and reestablished air pressure. Marc, who was behind the person he had just rescued, was anxiously monitoring the vital signs on the person's space suit. They had seemed hopeful in the cabin of the tug, and now the indications were certain: respiration and heartbeat were back.

"Saved!" the young man said jubilantly.

Once the lock had been properly pressurised, the door opened. Carl and other passengers crowded round. The survivor's suit was removed, and only then was it apparent that the survivor was a girl.

Vermasen and Marc unsuited while the girl slowly regained her spirits.

Later, after a cup of hot soup, she was able to say that she had been on a routine inspection of the tug when a terrible explosion had thrown her craft clear of the Nordri's hull.

Marc was warmly congratulated by both Vermasen and the pilot, and started to regain a little confidence in himself.

Chapter Eight
A Call in the Night

In the afternoon, Trevor MacKinnon went to inspect the northern bastion of the ramparts, but didn't notice anything suspicious. At suppertime, he brought it up with his young guests, reproaching them for having ignored the "Danger" sign. But his grand-daughter remained rather silent, knowing full well that the one responsible for the explosion had had all the freedom he needed to conceal the evidence. She now wondered if an attempt had really been made on their lives, or if someone had simply tried to frighten them. The conspirator could not see Cynthia and Francis in the guard-room, and consequently, couldn't have known when they'd be near to the chimney, if ever. Whether it was delayed or not, the explosion was intended, then, to destroy the fireplace, but not to harm the youngsters. The chances of killing them — both of them — were very slim. Besides, why would anyone want to kill them?

On the other hand, Cynthia understood very well why one would want to scare them: to discourage them from walking around in the castle, having them believe that it was dangerous, and that the vaulted ceilings could give in at any moment. What was it they didn't want them to know? Rather, who did they not want them to see? Gregory, the lunatic poet!

This was enough to make up her mind. She would talk to him. After the meal, Trevor MacKinnon suggested an after-dinner walk in the upper courtyard. Cynthia asked for another story, even if she knew them all. Trevor did not need to be coaxed.

The curse of the Transylvanian traveller, he told them, took on many different forms over the centuries. Among them, discord and treachery at the very heart of the MacKinnon dynasty. At the beginning of the 17th century, for example, the regency was assured by Mary MacKinnon, widowed for several years. She detested Sean, the first-born son of her husband from a previous marriage. As he was the eldest, he was to become heir to the crown when he came of age. But Mary wanted the youngest, her own son Robert, to be king.

She secretly hated Sean. The boy had only one guardian, the Baron Canmore, a vassal and friend of his dead father's. One day, after a long absence, Canmore came to the castle and asked to see Sean; he wanted to take him hunting as he sometimes did. Mary, the regent, told him that the boy had disappeared one morning with his valet, about a month before, and had not returned. The horses had been found, and the young valet had been strangled. Perhaps bandit highwaymen had kidnapped the prince and were holding him for ransom; but there had been no news at all.

The regent told him this in the courtyard, not wishing to receive Canmore in the throne room. But the baron was too disturbed to take offence. Dismayed and perplexed, he wondered why Sean had been so imprudent as to go hunting with a valet only for an escort. He suspected that Mary was lying, or not telling the whole truth.

At that moment, a metallic object was thrown onto the pavement of the courtyard. Canmore recognised the nielloed* iron plaque which ornamented the hunting bag he valued so much. One day when Canmore was out hunting with other nobles, a rival had tried to assassinate him from behind with a crossbow. But the projectile had struck one of the decorative plaques on his strap. It pierced the square plate, but Canmore received only a superficial wound. The traitor was punished and the baron kept the plaque — a talisman that had miraculously saved his life. Twenty years later, he had given it to Sean as a present, hoping that it would bring him luck as well.

And now the very object had been thrown at his feet. He recognised, unmistakably, its black enamel motifs, the diamond-shaped hole, the silver chain from which it hung. Ever since

Sean had received the gift, he had worn it every day, never taking it off. This made Canmore's suspicions clearer. He knew that Mary wanted the throne for her own son, Robert. With Sean gone, the youngest would become heir.

The baron seized the regent and held a knife to her throat. He ordered his men to take hold of the young Robert who was seen standing in a dungeon window. He was brought before Canmore who ordered him to kneel down and raised a sword to his neck. He demanded a confession from the regent, or else her favourite son would be killed. She admitted that under the upper courtyard, there were underground rooms connected to the dungeon cellars. Canmore went to inspect the cellar and found an old jailer who took him to the secret cells. The baron found Sean MacKinnon in one of these, pale, emaciated, but alive. Around his head was an iron frame, locked in place with a key, which made it impossible for him to move his jaw and call for help.

Once freed, Sean told of how the regent came down every day to torment him, demanding that he sign an abdication from the throne leaving his younger brother the heir. Free to move around the cell during the day, Sean had spent his time plotting his escape. The light from a basement window entered his cell through an oblique duct. This duct was barred at both ends. He had undertaken to loosen the bar closest to him. Patiently, by continually turning the bar, he had succeeded in making the opening large enough to break a fragment of the rock and pry the bar loose. This had made it possible for him to slide his body into the sloping duct.

The opening led to the moat surrounding the dungeon, just above the water level. It was in a corner, so that the window could almost not be seen by those in the courtyard.

Sean could only moan and no one could hear him among the hundreds of everyday castle noises. But that morning, he had heard Canmore's voice, and he heard the lies the regent was telling him. By squeezing himself up against the bars, he could even see the baron from behind. So in a desperate gesture, he had ripped off the precious pendant, and with his arm through the bars, hurled it as best he could toward Canmore, terrified that the plaque would fall in the water. But it fell onto the flagstones of the upper courtyard, and for this, Mary and the jailer were sentenced to death.

This is how Trevor MacKinnon finished his story. A few minutes ago they had stopped walking; like well-behaved schoolchildren, Cynthia and Francis sat at the foot of the stairs leading to the dungeon drawbridge; Trevor sat a few steps higher. During the story, dusk had settled in , and now, the only remaining light came from a few lanterns that went on automatically at nightfall.

His story finished, the General said goodnight to the youngsters and left. Nonetheless, it was still early, and Cynthia suggested to Francis that they take a walk along the parapet facing the sea.

The girl always kept a flashlight in her bag. There was electricity all over the castle but it didn't lend an air of mystery to things; she preferred not to light the lamps. Francis followed her through the hallways and stairways; but with the many detours, he had soon lost all sense of direction. The last staircase led outside onto the parapet walk between the west and north towers. On this side, the pointed roof of the chapel cut down to the middle of the curtain wall, but could be circumvented from the rear. The sea-breeze slapped against the youngsters' faces. On their right, as far as the eye could see, was the ocean, whereas on the left, was the estuary, growing narrower inland.

Cynthia and her friend walked quietly from one tower to the other, looking at the dungeon. Despite the drapes, a light could be seen coming through the windows of the last floor.

"That McSweeny is still watching us," said Francis.

From the side tower where he seemed to have his quarters, the General's secretary didn't hide the fact that he was watching them.

"If there's someone who doesn't like our being here," said Cynthia, "it's surely him. You'd think the castle belonged to him and that we were intruders."

"It's simple; we just have to pretend he isn't there."

Indeed, when they went behind the chapel roof, McSweeny could no longer see them.

At that moment, a metallic sound rang through the night. The youngsters started and turned around. The sound had come from the inner parapet only a few metres away. It was the sound of an object being thrown against stone. Immediately after, there was a clank on the roof of the living quarters, and then a sliding sound.

"Someone threw something at us."

"From the top of the dungeon maybe," said Cynthia.

In one of the windows facing them, the drapes were open; they had been closed only the moment before. But the inside was dimly lit now, and they couldn't see anyone. Cynthia considered pointing her flashlight toward the dungeon's terrace but she thought better of it. Her intuition told her not to. Instead she went to the parapet and shone her flashlight on the sloping roof of the living quarters, covered with chimneys.

"Can you see anything?"

But only the faded verdigris of the copper and the sombre brick was visible in the circle of light.

"There! A reflection!" There was a pale metallic reflection at the base of a chimney at the lower end of the roof.

"Let's go see."

"Are you crazy? We'll break our necks."

The roof had a 25-degree incline and the drop to the courtyard flagstones was about nine metres.

But already Cynthia had turned off her flashlight and had straddled the parapet. She leaned up against the chimney closest to her which was in line with the one she wanted to get to.

"Come and join me."

Francis followed her against his will. She explained what she wanted to do, given the shortage of rope. The distance was almost four metres. Their bodies, stretched out, were that long.

"The lower chimney will stop us if we slide," she insisted. "The worst that can happen is that we'll have to ask for help to get back up."

Francis started out, grumbling. He passed the first chimney and, without letting go of it, stretched out on his belly along the roof. Then Cynthia crawled down the roof hanging on to him, and then, crawling flat on her belly, and holding Francis's ankles, she touched the second chimney with her feet, the lowest one, the one against which the metallic object had stopped sliding.

Confident now, she reached for it and put it in her pocket. The hardest part was yet to come. She stretched out on her belly again, and grabbed hold of Francis' ankles — he served as a cable. Little by little she climbed back up, clutching his calves and thighs while he muttered and complained under his breath

"You're pinching me!"

But that wasn't the worst of it. He hugged the first chimney with his two arms, his face pressed against the rough surface. His hands and fingers slipped little by little over the edges of the rough bricks as Cynthia's weight pulled him unrelentingly downward.

Just as he felt himself sliding down, no longer able to hold on to the sides of the chimney, the traction stopped. His friend Cynthia had reached the first chimney, climbing up until she had a good footing. From her position, she helped Francis get around the chimney and get back to the parapet.

The youngster sat down, his hands raw, vowing never again to serve as a rope for an amateur mountain-climber. But Cynthia didn't listen to his recriminations.

"Look," she said, holding the object up to the light. It was a plaque, made of iron apparently, about the size of a playing card, with embossed motifs of black enamel. It had a diamond-shaped hole through which a silver chain was strung.

"Does it remind you of anything?"

"That's incredible!"

The good-luck charm that saved the imprisoned prince's life in grandfather MacKinnon's legend.

"But it was only a story."

"The dungeon is full of old things and my grandfather has a story for each one of them. I had already heard tonight's story, and this talisman was in a glass cabinet in the throne room."

"Where is it?"

"On the second floor of the dungeon."

They were silent for a moment, thinking.

"The talisman was thrown at us," said Francis finally, "as it was in the story."

"To call for our help."

"The regent, the wicked old lady, she had lied to Baron Canmuch.

"Canmore. I think grandfather lied to us too."

"About the loony poet?"

"Yeah."

She turned off her flashlight, and looked again towards the dungeon. The curtains were still open on the window. This time, though, they could see the head and shoulders of a man just behind the glass.

A blond head, that of the poet. He was looking at them.

"He must have heard the story grandfather was telling before," said Cynthia softly.

"From up there?"

"Maybe he's allowed onto the other floors. From the second floor he could have heard easily."

All of a sudden, Cynthia sensed that someone was watching them from the top of the watchtower.

"That must be Gregory's guard," the girl surmised. "I hope he didn't see him throwing this," she said, glancing down at the talisman.

"We could say that we dropped something on the roof."

And off they went to discuss this in more comfortable surroundings. One floor down, in the corridor, they discovered the lights on and heard a footfall. Cynthia recognised the sound of McSweeny's boots; he was coming to see what the youngsters were up to, no doubt, now he'd lost sight of them.

They started off in the opposite direction, hurrying through the shadowy castle. While McSweeny was looking for them on the roof, they were well on their way home to their rooms.

Chapter Nine
Deep in the Moon

As soon as they arrived on the Moon, Carl and Marc went to the Language School, where Argus agents received the rapid instruction necessary for their missions. For hours and hours they sat there, in an almost hypnotic state, wearing helmets equipped with speakers. At regular intervals one could hear them translating sentences, and their Russian improved rapidly. They were helped by a drug which stimulated the memory centres in the brain.

When it came time to go to bed, both of them had terrible headaches, but they would have been able to have a conversation with either Grigor or Niki Syeline.

The next morning, they no longer had headaches, but they retained everything they had learned. They would suffer some memory loss only after a few days.

From their room, a large rectangular porthole looked onto the black sky of the Moon.

"Come and see," said Carl, who was the first up. "There are some fighters doing training exercises above the crater."

Argus was built on the edge of the Tsi-olkovsky crater, one hundred and fifty kilo-metres across. The fighter pilots regularly came for manoeuvres above the lunar landscape, where there is a certain amount of gravity; not as much as on Earth, of course, so they also some-times practised around Venus, to familiarise themselves with how their crafts handled in the atmosphere.

Marc hurried to the window and located three moving points that Carl was showing him, just above the western crest of the crater. Three fighters; they had to belong to the cruiser Dagur, which was in orbit around the Earth.

They banked and came towards the centre of the crater, where there was a large mountain. They soon disappeared from Carl's and Marc's sight. Then, all of a sudden, they reappeared, plainly visible now, skimming the mountaintops and then rising diagonally in brilliant fashion. There was no sound, but the brightness of the flame spouting from their thrusters was enough to give a sense of their power. Long and tapered, equipped with flaps for atmospheric flight, they could intercept any bomber, fighter or even missile. When the fighter-carrier Thor was finally constructed, Argus would have the power to neutralise all the warring forces on Earth.

The machines disappeared, and Carl and Marc waited their return in vain. They had undoubtedly gone to pursue their training exercises farther away.

"Let's get some breakfast," Carl finally decided. "You've got to spend a couple of hours at the Training Centre."

Marc had to familiarise himself with the equipment used by Argus agents, and especially with that used for communication, shooting and self-defence. This was just in case he had to act side by side with Carl. More and more he seemed to accept the idea of a mission for Argus. If he was successful, he would feel he could be useful to the society which had so generously granted him asylum.

The boy knew little of the lunar city. He had only been there once, before his departure for Erymede, and the visit had been a brief one. On their way to the Operations sector, their route led Carl and his friend through a glassed-in corridor which overhung a deep well. It took Marc's breath away. As far as he could see, the well went on forever, dozens and dozens of floors down towards the centre of the Moon. All along the wall ran a multitude of tubes, cables, and fibre optic cables glowing in the shadows. Throughout all of this, there were hundreds of control apparatuses with panels studded with innumerable indicators and tiny lights. These were reached through a labyrinth of gangways and trellis balconies linked by ladders, as well as a number of elevators which seemed to move incessantly. But the most fascinating thing was the transparent pipes where energy was flowing in its pure state; very straight, bluish light

70

beams that came from the very depths of the city, under kilometres of rock.

And people were working in the wells, women and men dressed in protective uniforms. They must be, thought Marc, incredibly courageous to work in the middle of such a flow of brute energy. Marc didn't even want to think of what would happen if some accident broke a duct or caused a light beam to deviate.

The very speed of the elevators gave him vertigo, and he wasn't even sure whether he would dare get on one of them. The adventure he had had yesterday in space seemed a very modest one compared to the daily bravery of these technicians.

* * *

After several hours spent in the Training Centre, Carl and Marc went to Operations. Lea Laredo stood in front of a giant screen, featuring a map of north-western Europe, and briefed them on the latest developments in the Syeline story.

"Well, that's a coincidence!" Carl exclaimed after Laredo had finished her briefing.

"What's that?"

"I was on a mission in exactly that place just last year. There was a secret conference, and my job was to infiltrate and sabotage it."

"That makes things a lot easier, then."

"And how!"

First, the two friends had to get to the regional base in Norway. There, Carl would assemble two commando teams while Marc would dye his hair so he looked like Syeline's son. There was no definitive plan of action, and no one knew whether the look-alike trick would be used, but they had to be ready for anything.

A few minutes later, Carl and Marc boarded a shuttle leaving the Moon.

Chapter Ten
Deep in the Earth

"Oh, stop griping!" said Cynthia, impatient. She and Francis were going down the ravine that cut the promontory in two. At the bottom, the river ran in torrents. The foam, swirling around the rocks didn't help Francis's vertigo. The rock face was almost vertical.

The trail could barely be seen from the bridge. Once they got going, they realised that it was easy. For in spite of what Francis said, the path was easy. It went down along a gentle diagonal on the north side of the ravine to reach the river down from the bridge. There were ledges and stones in step formation and strongly rooted shrubs to hang on to. It was almost impossible to fall.

The youngsters finally set foot on the rocks bordering the torrent. The roar of the water was so loud that they almost had to yell at each other.

Looking up, they saw the stone bridge thirty or forty metres away and made out the towers of the barbican. No one seemed to have watched them come down. If it was the chauffeur's task to keep an eye on them, he certainly didn't seem to have orders to follow them — he couldn't do so without being seen, anyway.

"What next?" asked Francis, thinking to himself that he'd never agree to go back up by the same path.

Cynthia pointed out a crack in the cliff, that got larger toward the bottom. The water poured into the cavity with the rocks partially blocking the entrance. A cluster of thin saplings almost completely obscured the crevice.

"Part of the river passes under the cape and empties into the sea."

"Don't tell me we're going to have to dive in, now?"

"Of course not. Follow me."

Holding onto crannies in the rock face, Cynthia advanced to the crevice, put one foot in the water, then the other, and bent down to get through the opening.

"See, there's an underwater ledge and the water only goes to our thighs."

Francis followed her. Soon, they were in total darkness and he stopped to give his eyes time to adjust to it. The water on his legs felt icy cold and he was afraid of losing his footing and being carried away by the current.

Cynthia lit one of the powerful electric torches they had bought that morning in the village.

"Be careful," she said, "there are a few steps." Francis climbed those, and stepped onto a dry ledge beside a little underground river. Past the entrance, the roof of the cave was higher. The path was more or less flat, large enough for one person to walk along easily, ducking one's head occasionally where the roof slanted. The river, on the left, was a few metres wide and flowed gently. It wasn't too deep, according to Cynthia.

It was, she explained, one of the passages used by the residents when the castle was under siege. There were three routes, according to her: this one, another leading to the village, and a last one on the ocean side, at the foot of the cliff.

With their two lamps lit, Cynthia and Francis advanced quickly. To break the silence, Cynthia started to tell one of her grandfather's tales.

"Do you really have to?" protested Francis.

"Oh come on, they're only stories."

So she began with the story of how the MacKinnons had kept a dragon in the underground passages for centuries.

"A dragon!"

"Yes, a dragon. A dwarf dragon, which means that it was about the size of a horse. With large bat-like wings, and sinister crocodile eyes, and a mouth that spat fire."

"Naturally."

"One of my ancestors had brought it back from some voyage. He's said to have captured it on some rocky and deserted island in the north, torn by volcanoes. The dragon was young and almost harmless."

"It must have been a nuisance."

"He was allowed to roam free in the underground passages, guarding them."

"Good protection against surprise attacks!"

"A lair was made for him — a nest of sorts — in the cliff by the sea; a kind of grotto."

"Would the dragon stay in its nest?"

"Sometimes he'd escape and terrorise the shepherds in the fields around, or the fishermen in their boats."

"Did someone finally kill it?"

"No. The ancestor who captured and trained it was the only one who could approach it. When he died, nobody dared go down into the underground passages. According to the legend, the dragon is still there, hibernating in some crevice, waking up now and again to devour those bold enough to venture down into the passageways."

"That's a reassuring tale!"

Francis tried to listen to the silence; but in his ear there was only the occasional ebb and flow of the river. They came to a fork; a gallery on the right opened on the underground river tunnel.

"That passage there leads to the cellar of a house on the edge of the village."

The combined glow of their lamps revealed that the passage was blocked by a pile of rubble. Cynthia wasn't surprised. From year to year, she'd found more and more rocks on the ground here, and she'd suspected that the roof would eventually collapse.

The youngsters continued along beside the little river. After a bend in the tunnel, a faint light could be seen in the distance, a light that grew brighter as they drew closer.

The passage finally opened into a large cavern with a low roof. The river flowed into the cavern in cascades, forming a lake. On the other side, an almost vertical fissure let in the light of day, almost blinding them in the darkness.

"The overflow from the lake," explained Cynthia, "spills into the sea, at the bottom of the cliff. At the new moon, when the tide is high, the waves reach the cavern, giving the water in the castle wells a salty taste."

This lake, much larger than it looked, was the castle's underground reservoir. The water was drawn from bottomless wells."

"And nobody but you knows about this cavern?"

"Nobody, I believe. From a boat, this cave looks like one among a lot of other rock crevices. There's no way of guessing that there's a cavern here."

The ledge along the side of the lake led to a staircase chiselled right out of the rock. It led to a vertical chimney that opened up into a vaulted roof above the waterline. It spiralled up the chimney like the threads of a screw around the empty space in the centre.

"It's the dungeon well," explained the girl. "In the last century, you'd have seen a bucket on the end of a rope go down empty and come up full."

Francis marvelled at all the work involved in digging these wells. And in the Middle Ages! Tens and tens of metres of rock. It was a long climb. Francis walked close to the wall, staying as far away from the central well as possible. Finally, long before reaching the top, they saw an opening on the side. The staircase turned off, cutting into the rock and forming a large curve.

After several steps, they came to a kind of niche in the rock face. There were steps cut out of the rock at the back of the alcove, which led to a seemingly vertical chimney.

During part of the morning and afternoon, Cynthia and Francis had secretly watched the dungeon. They were sure now that someone was standing guard at all times on the first floor where the armoury was. From there, he could watch over the only door and stairway to the tower. Cynthia had thought of another route.

She went into the vertical shaft first, explaining: "One escape route wasn't enough for those who built all these passages. So they chose one of these dungeon chimneys and extended it down to here. The fireplaces were walled up and there's a trap door installed on each floor."

The shaft was narrow and their backs

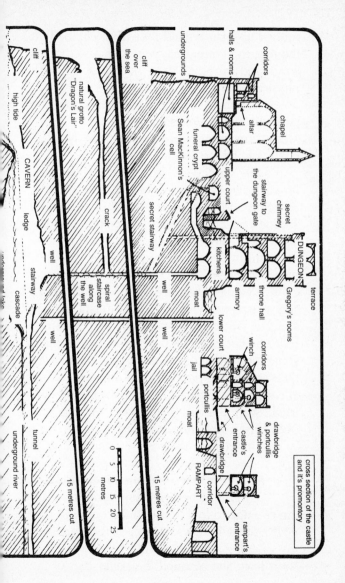

cross section of the castle and it's promontory

Top section (castle interior):

corridors

halls & rooms

undergrounds

chapel

altar

secret chimney

funeral crypt

Sean MacKinnon's cell

stairway to the dungeon gate

upper court

secret stairway

kitchens

throne hall

armory

DUNGEON

Gregory's rooms

terrace

drawbridge & portcullis winches

corridors

winch

jail

lower court

portcullis

moat

castle's entrance

drawbridge

corridor

RAMPART

rampart's entrance

15 metres cut

0 5 10 15 20 25
metres

Middle section:

cliff over the sea

crack

secret stairway

well

well

well

spiral staircase along the well

cascade

stairway

tunnel

underground river

15 metres cut

Bottom section (left):

cliff

high tide

CAVERN

ledge

natural grotto 'Dragon's Lair'

well

moat

underground lake

15 metres cut

rubbed up against the sides as they climbed. At the top, the youngsters were exhausted, their hands and arms sore; they weren't used to such physical effort.

"I hope you weren't wrong about the talisman," whispered Francis.

"I'm sure it was a call for help. Now be quiet, and let me listen."

She slipped into one of the cavities that, on each floor, gave access to the trap doors. Twisting and turning, she put her ear to the wooden trap door which was covered on the other side with a flagstone. Despite the thickness, she was sure she would hear voices, if there were any. There was complete silence.

"You're going to help me pull the trap," she whispered. The panel was meant to slide along a wooden rail with the help of small rollers. Anticipating this, Cynthia had brought some lubricating oil from the basement of the little house. She poured some onto the rollers, and then after listening again to the silence, she tried, with Francis' help, to open the trap door. "Just a bit," she suggested.

But it was impossible. Unmovable at first, the panel suddenly burst open — much more than "just a bit," making quite a noise.

Cynthia bit her lip. Then she mustered up the courage to look through the opening. She realised that there was a piece of furniture over the opening, and she could see between its short legs. She scanned the better part of the square hall that made up the second to last floor of the dungeon. And in this room, a man rose from his chair, intrigued by the noise at the trap door. He came closer, not sure of where the noise was coming from.

As far as Cynthia could tell, he was alone in the room. She reached into her pocket for the iron plaque and threw it in front of the piece of furniture. The metallic clinking sound caught the blond man's attention; he bent over to pick up the talisman, with an incredulous look on his face.

Cynthia pulled on the chain which she hadn't let go of. The little plaque skitted along under the piece of furniture, indicating to Gregory where his rescuers were.

"It's you?" he whispered, crouching down in front of the piece of furniture.

"Yes, we got your message."

"That's extraordinary! How did you ever get under a dresser?"

"I know the castle well enough."

"That's what I hoped. But through the floor of my room.!"

"You're being held prisoner here?"

"I believe so. Up until yesterday, I wasn't sure, but now..."

He spoke English with an accent that Cynthia didn't recognise immediately.

"I mean, they didn't lock you up because you're crazy?"

"That's what they told you?"

81

"My grandfather did, yes. But he's a poor liar."

"The old man is your grandfather?"

"Yes, but don't worry. I'm not his accomplice."

"I want to believe you. I know they wish you weren't here"

"Who?"

"The guards, the military. Especially the officer who threw the grenade at you."

"A grenade?"

Yesterday morning, on one of the rampart's bastions. He threw a grenade into the chimney, and..."

But Gregory was interrupted by a voice which seemed to Cynthia to come from far away. In a split second, she saw a look of worry and fear come over the prisoner's face.

"Greg," announced the voice, "it's suppertime."

Without hesitation, the blond man replied, "I don't give a damn; everything you cook tastes bad anyway."

At the same time, he ripped the knob from his watch.

"Oh, you're in a bad mood today," the voice said, coming into the room. "But what are you doing?"

"You'd be in bad humour too," answered Gregory, "if you'd just broken the winder off your watch. Luckily I found it again." He showed it to his visitor, one of the guards undoubtedly, the tiny silver knob he pretended to have found on the floor. The guard didn't appear to suspect anything.

Gregory walked to the door with him and remained out of sight for a long time. Finally he returned and knelt down beside the chest of drawers, keeping a close eye on the door.

"I can't talk to you any longer. If I don't go down to eat they'll come for me. But return tonight, if you can."

"Will you tell us why you've been locked up here?"

"Yes, it's a long story. But leave now; it would be a shame if you were caught."

He rose and walked over to the open door to check if anyone had overheard him.

Cynthia, leaving the trap door open, climbed down to where Francis stood. They heard a last muffled "thank you" from Gregory and that was all.

* * *

The youngsters were in the tunnel once again, this time walking in the opposite direction. Cynthia was haunted by Gregory's face, his blue eyes filled with despair and fear. He was older than she had first thought, forty maybe, judging from the wrinkles around the eyes. His rather long blond hair, and his clean-shaven face had fooled her at a distance. But that didn't

83

change Cynthia's feelings about him. Because she had a feeling about him which was more than just sympathy. Though she reasoned with herself, though she told herself she was acting like a heroine in a romance novel, she couldn't escape her feeling. Was is because she felt the need to protect him, to help him? Would she feel so drawn to him if he weren't a prisoner, lost and helpless?

Francis put his hand on her arm, interrupting her thoughts.

"Did you hear that?" whispered the boy.

He pointed the flashlight towards the tunnel that led to the village. There was no one there, no one between them and the rockslide. And yet Francis was sure he had heard... he wasn't quite sure what — maybe voices. But they had been far away and somehow shapeless. It had been impossible to make out a phrase or even a word distinctly. Impossible, even, to know whether someone had been speaking at all.

While Cynthia listened, it happened again. The acoustics in the tunnels was such that the voices seemed to come out of nowhere. They were disembodied mumblings, voices born out of the blackness.

They were the voices of phantoms.

Without a word, Cynthia and Francis hurried away towards the exit.

Chapter Eleven
The Syeline-Scott Operation

Back on Earth again.

Marc had thought he would be more emotional about it. Maybe it was because it wasn't his own country.

The Norwegian forest, which opened up to allow the shuttle access to the regional base, hadn't awakened any sense of belonging in Marc. Even less had the blue-grey waves of the North Sea which foamed beneath the belly of the helicopter.

Now he looked down at this little fishing village, the ill-matched houses; some trawlers were moored at the mouth of the river. The wind brought the smell of fish and the shrill cries of seagulls. The twilight shadows darkened all colour, and only the eastern sky shone — with a breathtaking blue.

The young man felt like he was on holiday. That was it: a visit to a strange country, a pretty country but otherwise nothing special. A few kilometres off shore, there was perhaps at this very moment a drilling platform or a tanker spilling black death onto the ocean. To the south, the industrial cities spewed opaque fumes skyward that would return to earth as acid rain. For Marc, this was Earth: a planet conquered and occupied by irresponsible people.

The young man shook himself. Against the likes of that, not even Argus could do much. Today though, Marc had a very specific mission to accomplish, and it would be better if he concentrated on that. He was still amazed at the foresight with which Carl had prepared the operation during their stop at the regional base. Andersen seemed to have foreseen everything; at every step of the way, he had a solution if something were to go wrong. Marc never dreamed that this sort of mission would involve so much equipment and so many agents.

The operation had hit a snag even before it began. A minor obstacle, at least so one hoped, otherwise things would be more complicated. Carl had ordered the material and men necessary to eliminate the obstacle from the regional base. The most delicate part of the mission was to get this equipment into the little house without attracting too much the attention of the villagers. The cottage was at some distance from the village but, because it was normally deserted, any sort of activity would be noticed.

"All right, it's time."

Marc turned around: Carl Andersen had just come out of the porch, dressed in Earth fashion with clothes he had chosen at the regional base.

"It doesn't bother you too much to stay here?" asked Andersen.

"A bit, but it's necessary."

And Marc wasn't alone: Phan Vihn and Kati Vogel were downstairs, setting up the communications network they would need during the mission.

And again Marc felt as though he was useless; he was the one born on Earth, but it was Carl who knew how to drive a car.

"You remember? The main thing is not to act suspiciously. If a villager approaches you, don't hide — on the contrary, talk to him; use my assumed name and explain that you're on vacation with me. I actually own this cottage under my assumed name, so everything is in order."

Marc nodded, watching his friend get on the light van parked under the porch roof which flanked the cottage.

The vehicle started and then moved off up the sloping road, its headlights peering into the oncoming night. Marc felt all alone on Earth, and, once again, the idea occurred to him that he was going to be abandoned there.

* * *

The second van was already at the rendezvous point when Carl arrived. He got down and talked with the other man, an Earth auxiliary, an agent to whom the true nature of the Argus Organisation had not been revealed. He thought he was working for a secret service related to the United Nations.

The moor was deserted, and utterly silent under a moon already high in the sky. There wasn't a village, not even a hamlet, for as far as the eye could see. There wasn't a car on this lonely road.

Then there was a noise, a rhythmic droning together with a faint whine. The helicopter from the regional base, flying very close to the ground, arrived suddenly; it was extremely fast and almost silent compared to Earth's helicopters.

Without landing lights of any sort, the machine lightly touched ground with the precision of its automatic pilot. Several men and women disembarked and busied themselves noiselessly with transferring some equipment from the helicopter to the vans. Everything seemed light to them, and in less than half an hour the job was done.

The helicopter then left discreetly, another of its clandestine missions accomplished.

Chapter Twelve
The Dragon

The moon, now in its first quarter, shone brightly, making Cynthia and Francis' descent into the ravine less hazardous. But the brightness had its disadvantages — it made them more visible. Cynthia hoped that the chauffeur responsible for supervising them would not look out his window in the tower beside the ravine.

At night, the climb down took longer than it had this afternoon. The girl was impatient, thinking of Gregory who was perhaps already waiting for them in his dungeon.

They finally reached the rocks at the edge of the torrent. The moonlight didn't reach the bottom of the ravine, so they had to use their flashlights to make their way through the entrance to the tunnel.

Inside the tunnel nothing had changed since the afternoon; the darkness was the same. But there was a cause for anxiety that hadn't been there before: the mystery of voices heard at the juncture of the galleries. Did Trevor MacKinnon know about these passageways?

Would he have posted guards there, or had them patrolled? In which case, the "poet" being held there had much more significance than he was willing to admit.

Suddenly, the youngsters stopped. A faint, low-pitched crackling or sputtering sound echoed in the distance. They looked at each other in the dim light of their flashlights. Obviously, these secret passages were not as quiet as Cynthia had thought.

"We must find out what it is," decided Cynthia. They continued on. On their left, the water flowed in silence, except for the odd gurgle.

Then, a few minutes later, the sound echoed again; it seemed closer now, a kind of throbbing drone. This time the girl signalled to Francis to turn off his flashlight.

But before their eyes could adjust to the dark, another light started to shine. It came from beyond one of the curves in the tunnel, outlining the slanted roof of the cave, the ledge which served as a path, and the black water running below. The light had a red glow with an occasional orange glare.

There was smoke as well; they could see it and smell it; the acrid odour of something overheating or burning. It wasn't a familiar smell and they could not imagine what was burning.

And the noise... like a furnace with an occasional muffled crackling sound. The thought occurred to Cynthia and Francis both at once: the dragon! The mighty dragon responsible for guarding the underground passageways, the dragon who had outlived his master, and who went on haunting the tunnels.

"It's impossible," said Francis, in a hushed voice. "It doesn't exist, it never has."

Cynthia agreed with him, and she decided that to continue on once the noise had stopped and the light went out. Francis turned on his flashlight again, aiming the light at the ground, making it less visible.

A dragon, in the twentieth century? Impossible; they lived only in fairy tales and legends.

The two youngsters moved along, repeating these reasonable and logical arguments to themselves while the acrid odour irritated their throats more and more as they advanced. The heat too was becoming more and more oppressive.

Then suddenly, on the right, the light flashed again; and then the noise, a furious sputtering roar punctuated by high whistling sounds. A glare of light or flames filled the passageway, illuminating the smoke which was shot through with sparks.

Cynthia and Francis jumped backwards. It was all coming from the tunnel linked to the underground river.

Then all hell broke loose. With one deafening roar, a huge, bright red flame shot through the tunnel, discharging a cloud of acrid smoke. Sparks and melting debris spewed forth as if from a machine gun, sending up little geysers of whistling steam as they plunged in the water.

Blinded, their faces and hands burnt, the youngsters made an about-face and fled, their coughing inaudible in the uproar. But the roaring soon stopped and all they could hear was the sound of falling rocks and the furious hissing steam. Their eyes tearing and half-choking, Cynthia and Francis ran away, zigzagging, with their flashlights leading the way.

Their main concern was not to fall in the river, as they tried to forget about the flame, the terrible flame which could have engulfed them and thrown them against the other rock face, burnt to a cinder, had they been a few metres closer.

* * *

The exit was far away, giving them time to recover from their panic. Nobody was chasing them. Nothing was coming after them.

They came to the narrow exit. Francis, in a hurry to get out, lost his footing on the submerged rocks and fell into the water. Cynthia, in an effort to keep him from falling, also lost her balance and followed him into the black, icy water.

But the underground arm of the river wasn't deep, and feeling the bottom with their feet, they got up, steadying themselves against the current. Standing, the water reached their shoulders.

The coldness of the water had a calming effect.

"I lost my flashlight," said Francis.

Cynthia had almost lost hers too but she had had the instinct to throw it behind her as she fell. She felt around the ledge just inside the passage and finally came across an object. She felt around for the switch, shook the light until it flickered. The glass was cracked, but otherwise, they had merely to readjust the battery and tighten the bulb for the flashlight to work again.

The youngsters came out of the water into the open air. The sound of the torrent unnerved Francis. "We mustn't stay here; we wouldn't hear whatever is in the tunnel if it decided to come out."

They began their upward climb. But the moon was no longer there to light the way along the ledge of the ravine: it must have gone for the night. And with only the one flashlight, it was a long, slow climb. Half-way, Cynthia stopped.

"We're being ridiculous."

The fall in the icy water and the fresh night air had brought her to her senses.

"Let's sit down for a minute. We're safe here."

Exhausted, Francis agreed to take a break to catch his breath. But he looked worriedly at the entrance to the tunnel below them. The acrid smell of smoke was still in his hair, that thick smoke that had almost suffocated them. He could still feel his hands and face smarting from the light burns which the water had soothed momentarily.

Cynthia turned off their one flashlight to save the batteries; the light of the stars would be enough.

"Dragons don't exist," she affirmed. "They simply do not exist. There has to be another explanation."

"You heard the roaring just as I did," protested Francis, "And the flame. It went through the pile of rubble blocking the tunnel. Do you know of anything that can destroy tons of rock without an explosion?"

"No, but we'll find out."

"Anyhow, I'm not going back down there."

Chapter Thirteen
The Laser

The basement of the little cottage had been transformed into a control room; there were television screens, control panels, and two technicians. A length of large flexible tubing lay across the floor as well as a fire hose and several electrical cables. There were about ten people crowded into the basement of this little house which until yesterday had been deserted.

Putting his head next to a basement window through which was blowing a strong wind, Carl called to someone outside.

"The smoke wasn't too visible?" he asked.

"Hardly at all. You were right to wait for the moon to go down."

Carl walked over to the technicians seated by the controls. One of the screen showed a part of a tunnel starkly illuminated by floodlights. The other showed the same scene, but this time in infrared, so that the rocks at the end of the tunnel glowed a greenish white.

"The gasses are entirely cleared," announced one of the technicians, after checking the equipment. "We're continuing to ventilate the area."

"The temperature?"

"Tolerable in the tunnel. The stones are still red-hot."

"The reservoir is full again?"

"Yes, but this is the last time. The well for the house is dry."

"Turn on the water."

A white stream appeared on the television, which immediately turned into steam. The monitors transmitted the hissing that came as the cold water showered down on the burning stones.

The flexible tubing expanded a little, bringing the steam to the chimney of the cottage, where it poured out into the night over the sleeping village. It would have been too risky to do that if the moon had been shining.

Then the water reserve was dry, and the ventilator had emptied the tunnel of all steam. Carl made up his mind.

"It's time."

Followed by Marc and Helma, the engineer sent by the regional base, Carl slid through the trap-door in the floor of the basement and went down a steep staircase littered with cables and pipes.

In the tunnel there was a strong breeze because fresh air was being pumped in to replace the hot air that the ventilators were continuously clearing.

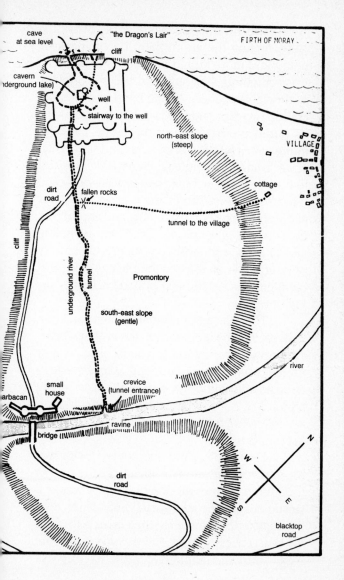

cave
at sea level

"the Dragon's Lair"

FIRTH OF MORAY

cliff

cavern
(underground lake)

well

stairway to the well

north-east slope
(steep)

VILLAGE

cottage

dirt
road

fallen rocks

tunnel to the village

cliff

underground river

tunnel

Promontory

south-east slope
(gentle)

river

small
house

crevice
(tunnel entrance)

barbacan

ravine

bridge

dirt
road

N

W

E

S

blacktop
road

97

The three Erymeans advanced with difficulty, feeling the atmosphere becoming ever hotter and more humid. In front of them there was something — a light that became brighter as they approached. At one bend, they almost couldn't go on; a large collapsible reservoir with its pump blocked almost the entire passage, along with a number of cameras and spotlights. There was a squat little machine which looked like a snowblower, but in reality was a powerful mining machine. Then there was the ventilator at the end of the flexible tubing, and another set of cameras, all equipped with thermometers and sensors. And most importantly, the battery of laser mini-cannons on their teleguided guncarriage which had been pulled back after firing.

This was the equipment which had been delivered by helicopter from the regional base, a fraction of the might of Erymede, but sufficient to clear a seemingly insurmountable obstacle in minutes. But although it took the lasers only minutes to cut through the rock, it had taken several hours for the preparations and security precautions.

Here the ground was covered with water, and condensation dripped from the roof of the tunnel. The smell of molten rock was still strong despite the attempt to ventilate. As they approached, the three felt their faces burn with the heat of the hot rocks. Helma approached the metal bars which supported the roof a couple of meters in front of the debris. They were props put in place with the help of the mining machine, before the lasers were fired, to stop other pieces of rock from falling into the space which had been cleared. They had done their job; only a few stones had broken away from the ceiling.

To each bar, one by one, Helma connected an apparatus she had brought with her. A tiny monitor gave a read-out of the each bar's torsion and the pressure each was under at the moment.

After several calculations on her integrated micro-computer, she said, "The rock is stable for the moment. But I won't guarantee anything beyond forty-eight hours. Then we'll need stronger props."

"We'll know later on tonight if that will be necessary," Carl replied. "As for now, call your agents and get started on evacuating the material."

He went with Marc into the passage which had been cleared; there were still some stones in the way, some which had partially melted and were now resolidifying.

Stepping quickly over the burning stones, Marc had the impression he was crossing a furnace. He remembered the volley of scarlet beams he had seen on the television screen as the laser fired, the white-hot stone, crackling as it reached fusion and bursting in all directions. It was only a tiny fraction of the energy used, for instance, to dispose of the asteroids which would otherwise have collided with Erymede. But it was enough to vaporise anyone who might have been in the tunnel.

Beyond the obstacle, Carl and Marc stood at the edge of the underground river.

"We'll go with the current," said Carl.

"You're sure you know which way to go?"

"I explored all these passages last year. Without them, I would never be able to complete my mission. No one in security services knows about them, not even the old general who owns the castle."

Then they started, each carrying on his belt an assortment of tiny devices which were indispensable to their expedition. They knew nothing of the dragon that legend said haunted the underground network of the castle.

Chapter Fourteen
The Truth about Gregory

It was late at night when Francis finally agreed to go down to the underground river again. Cynthia hadn't given him a convincing explanation — only hypotheses — but she did persuade him that it couldn't have been a dragon.

Once beyond the narrow entrance, they turned off their flashlight and listened. No sound came from the tunnel; there was no light either. They moved ahead with extreme caution, and were anxious; at any moment a flame could shoot through a fissure in the rock and engulf them. Without realising it, they went beyond the area where they first heard the sounds. Still nothing suspicious.

A little further, however, they stopped, their hearts beating wildly: sounds. But not at all the same ones as before. A banging, metallic thuds, voices. And with a closer look: a bluish-white glow.

The dragon-like roaring and sputtering was gone, it had disappeared.

"Let's move on a bit," whispered Cynthia.

Francis followed her, relieved in spite of himself. At least the light and the sounds were those of men and not of some ancient monster.

They came to a bend where they thought they saw a spot of light on the rock face; they guessed where it was coming from.

"It's coming from the tunnel that leads to the village."

The voices too: the voices of two women and a man who spoke a language that neither Francis nor Cynthia could understand. The important thing was that they were human.

Suddenly the light faded, and all they could see was a dim, shifting glow.

The youngsters plucked up their courage and headed for the fork in the tunnel. The first thing they noticed was that the fallen boulders had disappeared, but they could smell the heat and acrid odour that lingered in the rocks. And in the distance, silhouettes disappearing around a bend, carrying heavy, cumbersome objects. The faint light from their flashlights revealed a squat machine partially blocking the tunnel. And then, utter darkness.

"How could they have done that?" exclaimed Cynthia who understood immediately. Then she asked herself who "they" were.

"They would have had to..."

Francis stopped in mid-sentence. He wasn't sure what it would have taken to clear the rubble and brace the roof, but he knew that it couldn't be done without explosives and heavy machinery, in such a narrow tunnel. *Unless they used lasers,* his imagination told him; but he rejected that idea immediately; no existing laser was powerful, compact and portable enough.

But that would explain the "dragon" effect so well.

Cynthia was aware of all that, but what was uppermost in her mind was who these people were and why had they come there. In any case, they didn't seem to want to use the passageway they had cleared.

"Let's hurry," she said, fearing that their mission to save the poet might be jeopardised.

"And what if they follow us?"

"There are enough passageways for us to hide from them."

They hurried along, lighting the way with their one flashlight.

* * *

With her head in the trap door opening, under the piece of furniture, Cynthia could distinguish something moving in the darkened room, that someone was kneeling close to the dresser.

"It's you?" murmured the prisoner.

"Yes, it's us. My name is Cynthia. And this is Francis."

Opening the trap a bit more, as quietly as

possible, Francis got his head through also, so that their heads were side by side.

"I don't see you but I think that you are very brave children."

"Braver than you think," remembered the boy anxiously.

"My grandfather told us that you were one of his cousin's sons, that you were a poet, and that your name was Gregory."

"I am not Scottish, but Russian. I am not a poet; I am a neurologist. And my name is Grigor Syeline."

Then he told them the whole story; crouched over, he seemed to speak to the floor, while they, squeezed together in a narrow vertical opening, listened.

* * *

"We can help you escape," said Cynthia. Tomorrow night: we'll tie up the chauffeur and take his car. I can drive; I'll bring it to the river bank, at the entrance to the ravine; there's a path there. During that time, Francis will come for you and will lead you to the exit. We could reach Inverness by 1:00 a.m. and be in Glasgow before dawn. We could contact Amnesty International in the morning; they may know some honest journalists; once your case gets some publicity, the military will leave you alone."

Grigor did not answer immediately. He

seemed hesitant. Then he said at last, "No, no I can't. They are holding my son. They could hurt him."

"But you just told us that he was in Stockholm, that they were waiting for the right moment to bring him quietly into Great Britain."

"They told me that a week ago. Sweden is close by and it's a neutral country; the KGB could not prevent Niki from travelling with a British or Scandinavian airline."

"He's a prisoner too, then?"

"Certainly. I even suspect that he is being held here in this castle."

"Impossible."

"Why impossible? This castle is enormous. Have you visited all the towers, all the tunnels, in the three days that you've been here?"

The girl could not answer. There were indeed many places in the castle where another prisoner could be hidden.

Since the first day, Cynthia's attention had been centred on the dungeon, but there were five towers and large sections of the castle she hadn't been to since her arrival.

Would her grandfather Trevor keep a child prisoner? Until yesterday she would have thought not, but today... This would explain the protests she heard the first day. Trevor was not happy with his role as jailer, but he obeyed orders. His new assistant, McSweeny, might have been hired to keep an eye on him and report any weaknesses to his superiors.

"What's your son's name, again?"

"Niki," he said, taking out a wallet to show Cynthia a picture.

"Well, we'll look for Niki. I grew up in this castle, and if someone is hidden here somewhere, I'll find him."

* * *

The girl and her friend went down the length of the secret chimney in silence. The vertical shaft opened on a stairway which lead to the well. Francis went down the steps first. He felt a needle-like jab in the left buttock, but as he reached back to feel the spot, the sensation was gone. Cynthia emerged from the chimney after him. She grabbed her left hip, having felt the same sensation herself.

She pointed her flashlight beam down the stairs, then up the stairs. Did something move up there? She listened; no noise, not even the most furtive sliding sound. Nothing suspicious in the pale circle of light; the batteries were getting low.

"Let's go," whispered Cynthia.

They went down to the well, then took the staircase that wound like the thread of a screw. Half-way down, the girl whispered to her friend to stop. She listened again to the silence, her flashlight out now. She thought she heard a sound coming from the top of the well, perhaps the sound of a footfall on steps. But once again, she seemed to have been mistaken.

"Do you think we're being followed?"

"I don't know."

She turned the flashlight on again, holding it at arm's length to try and catch someone by surprise, but she couldn't see anybody as far as the light carried. They continued their descent, as silently as possible, filled with fear of meeting up with something unpleasant.

But they reached the cavern without incident, and once again felt free to talk — in a subdued voice, however.

"Your grandfather," said Francis, "will never speak to you again if you help this man escape."

"I realise that, and it's a serious business. He also risks losing his rank as a General, if not worse."

They reached the tunnel with the underground river.

"But I can't be my grandfather's accomplice in this affair. They tricked poor Grigor, helped him to flee his country just to hold him prisoner here."

Francis decided that they could not remain passive faced with this situation. But he would have preferred a less exciting holiday.

* * *

When Carl and Marc came back through the tunnel that led to the village, all that remained in the passageway was the little rock drill.

"I hope they didn't notice it," remarked Andersen. It's enough that they think they're being followed."

"But since you want to make contact with them..."

"In an atmosphere of trust, yes. But for the moment, they must not know that there are others involved. If so, they will cancel their escape plan."

Walking at a good pace, the two Erymeans soon got to the cottage's cellar. The digging equipment was not to be moved without orders from Carl. Anderson decided first to contact Argus.

He and Marc got rid of their equipment; the infra-red visors and high-sensitivity microphones with which they were able to pick up the conversations between Grigor and his young rescuers, the pistol which Carl had used to fire anaesthetic darts at the guards and the micromarkers at Syeline, Cynthia and Francis.

Carl sat at the sound board and surveillance console. He contacted, on Argus, the Operations Service to which he must report. Lea Laredo appeared on the video screen. Carl summarised the events of the night.

"We may have a solution to the problem of trust we've spoken about," said Carl. Instead of approaching Syeline ourselves and wasting valuable time winning his trust, we'll let the two youngsters plan his escape."

"They're amateurs," protested Lareda.

"We'll help them, of course."

"And how will you win *their* confidence?"

"I don't know yet, but it should be easy."

As he spoke, he transmitted the photographs of Cynthia and Francis to Argus, pictures taken in the darkness of the underground passages, while Carl marked them with his microscopic projectiles.

"The girl is very ingenious," he added.

"You know her?"

"I worked here last fall, don't forget."

He looked at the locating system's large monitor on which the computer showed a three-dimensional map of the castle and its surroundings. Two luminous dots pinpointed the positions of Cynthia and Francis, another gave Grigor Syeline's location. Without knowing it, they were carrying the markers that Carl fired at them, in their flesh.

"In the meantime, we've located, photographed and radioscoped the frigate on which Niki Syeline is being held prisoner."

A map of the North Sea replaced the image of Lea Laredo.

"It is situated between the Orkney Islands and the Shetlands. A special team is on alert at the regional base in Norway. They're waiting for your orders."

"Good. From our end, we're still contemplating our next move. I'll put you up to date as soon as a decision is made."

Carl broke off communication and said to Helda, "You can send back your team. The fewer people there are around, the less suspicious we'll be in the eyes of the villagers. You stay there with the drilling machine, though; that tunnel is indispensable to us."

Then he turned back towards Marc, who had looking over Carl's shoulder as he talked with Lea Laredo.

"All we need now is a plan of action. Got any ideas?"

Chapter Fifteen
Prisoners

Cynthia and Francis started their investigation early; they were too nervous to sleep, and they left the cavern at dawn. They disguised the true purpose of their visit; Cynthia pretended to be showing her guest the ingenuity of mediaeval architects. They went down into the castle cellars, and came to the area where prisoners were kept in the times when the MacKinnons feuded with the neighbouring clans.

"Here," said Cynthia. "This was the guard room."

She pointed to two narrow corridors.

"On each side, there were cells. At the end of that passage was the torture chamber. At the end of this one was the common jail."

"There's no guard," said Francis. "The boy can't be here."

"Maybe he's so well hidden that they don't think he needs a guard. It's less obvious that way."

"All right. So where do we start?"

"Let's try the jail."

So they took the left corridor. There were no windows down here, not even small ones. They had two flashlights with fresh batteries. As they went by each open door, they pointed their light into the cells. All were deserted.

"Well, somebody's been here," Cynthia said under her breath. "This grate always used to be down."

She was referring to the portcullis at the entrance to the jail, a room with a vaulted ceiling and rusty chains riveted into the walls.

They took a couple of steps into the room, probing every nook and cranny with their flashlights.

"No," Cynthia decided, "nobody has been held here for centuries."

But a metallic crash erased the end of her sentence. Both Cynthia and Francis jumped, literally, and turned around. The portcullis had fallen shut, locking the room.

Their hearts beating, they rushed to the grate and shook it, but it didn't budge. Putting down their flashlights, they tried to lift the thing. A portcullis being an extremely heavy lattice of vertical and horizontal iron bars, they didn't manage to lift it even one centimetre.

"I don't understand," cried Cynthia. "We should at least be able to move it a bit."

"It must be jammed. Where is the pulley?"

Cynthia picked up her flashlight again.

"You see those two chains that go all the

way along the ceiling? They're attached to the winches I showed you in the guard room."

"But what made the grate fall?"

"The breaking mechanism on the winches must have failed."

"Just at the time we were visiting the prison?"

The girl didn't say anything. She didn't believe it was an accident either. The portcullis had always been kept closed, and then today it was mysteriously open, only to drop shut again behind their backs.

"I was so stupid not to be on my guard," cursed Cynthia, hitting the portcullis with the palm of her hand. "Now we'll be prisoners for hours, may for the entire day."

"We could yell for help, couldn't we?"

"Did you see how thick the guard room door was? And anyway, this wing is uninhabited. There's only the porter, and he's two floors above us."

"Let's try anyway."

She didn't respond, but shone her flashlight along the corridor to the point where it got lost in the darkness. Nothing was moving, and there was no noise from the guard room. Nevertheless, someone had followed them there, someone who maybe would not be satisfied with merely imprisoning them.

* * *

The cellars of the castle were totally dark; the prisoners had turned off their flashlights. They were crouching by the portcullis, their voices unsteady, their hopes low.

"It had to be McSweeny, it had to be," hissed the young girl. "He thought we were too curious. He didn't succeed in scaring us off the first time, so now he decided to just cut us off."

"But for how long? He wouldn't let us die of thirst?!"

Cynthia hoped not. But she wasn't convinced.

"A day, maybe a day and a half?" she said.

"Your grandfather will miss us long before then. He'll start a search."

"Yes. But if McSweeny tells him that he saw us *outside,* by the ravine or by the cliffs, for instance, grandfather won't look for us in the cellars."

"But then, he might never even find us?!"

Cynthia thought about it. Would McSweeny have the nerve to let MacKinnon's granddaughter die right here in his castle? The daughter of the British consul in Montreal? She didn't think so, or he would have done it already when he had the chance. On the other hand, Cynthia had something else to worry about. Would they take advantage of this to remove Niki, and even Grigor, because the castle was no longer a secure hiding place? Then there wouldn't be any way of saving them. The feeling Cynthia had for the man had grown since yesterday. He was now a fascinating figure to her, so intelligent and so naïve at the same time, resigned and yet ready to sacrifice himself for his son. She could picture herself escaping with him, sharing his anguish and then the joy of his deliverance.

The hours passed, and Cynthia's optimism lessened. Sure that they would be found eventually, she felt her present predicament was just something to be lived through. But when she began to get thirsty, the girl started to think that this was a very bad something to have live through, a real psychological torture. And she started to think that maybe, after all, McSweeny would indeed let them die there, letting time erase all trace of his deed.

Francis, for his part, was already plunged into the blackest despair. He was thinking of all the prisoners who had languished in this dungeon through the centuries, of those who died chained to these damp walls and who maybe even still haunted the darkness.

A sliding sound in the corridor made him start. He clenched his hand round his flashlight but didn't dare turn it on.

The silence fell again. The boy felt that Cynthia too had tensed.

There was another sound, closer this time. Rustling, sliding, noises barely audible but inevitable from someone trying to walk silently.

"Did you hear that?" whispered the young woman.

"Yes."

"Get your flashlight ready."

They could barely hear each other, they were talking so softly, but they understood each other perfectly. Their flashlights were both pointed towards the corridor.

"Now," whispered Cynthia.

After hours in the darkness, the light was dazzling. But in the corridor there was no one. Nothing.

Nothing? But what was that fleeting movement in the beam of their flashlights? That transparent form, that silhouette less than a shadow?

Francis leaped up and away, terrified. A ghost, the ghost of a prisoner, or maybe of one who had been executed; wasn't it coming from the torture chamber at the other end of the corridor?

Cynthia had also straightened herself up in order to face the danger.

"Don't be afraid," said a voice in English.

And suddenly a man appeared, there where until a second ago there had been merely a suggestion of his presence. He was fairly young, with brown hair, and was dressed in contemporary clothes. But he was carrying equipment one would expect only in a NASA laboratory; he was wearing a headset that included a microphone and what looked like flat, compact binoculars, and on his belt he had an unidentified apparatus which covered half his waist from his stomach to his back, and even more equipment.

"I frightened you," the man said, excusing himself. "This equipment produces an optic distortion which makes one almost invisible." He put his hand on the rather bulky machinery he was wearing around his waist. "It's just physics; advanced physics, if you will."

Advanced! Like the laser that obliterated the rock in the tunnel, thought Francis immediately.

The man raised the infrared visor which had enabled him to see in the dark. They could see his eyes, and his face inspired confidence; he had an caring smile. He approached the gate. Cynthia didn't move; the man had riveted her attention and she stared at him, knitting her eyebrows, as though she were trying to remember something.

"Who are you? I'm sure I've seen you somewhere before, and yet... I just can't remember where."

"I don't think so," he responded, but it wasn't really an answer.

Then, without preamble, he said, "You and I are after the same thing — rescuing Grigor Syeline. Putting him beyond the reach of those who covet his knowledge, so that he can live in peace."

Then he interrupted himself. "But you must be thirsty."

He took a flask from his belt, uncorked it and handed it to Cynthia between the bars of the portcullis.

"Don't drink it!" yelled Francis, stepping quickly towards her.

But it was too late.

"What did you think it was?" said Cynthia. "It's only fruit juice."

She handed the flask to her friend. It was fresh and very thirst-quenching; it even relieved hunger a little bit. The boy hesitated. But the stranger, not paying any attention to his lack of trust, went on.

"After his misadventures with the NATO agents, Grigor Syeline may be suspicious of me. So, I want to help you succeed in your plan for escape."

Cynthia, who had not, at any rate, lost her critical powers, squinted and asked, "And why should we trust you?"

"That's true," said the man, nodding his head. "Let's start by getting you out of there."

He strode back towards the guard room, disappearing around a corner. A light went on. They could hear clanking, the noise of chains.

"You pull too," shouted the man. "Pull the gate up."

The youngsters put down their flashlights, and grabbed one of the horizontal bars. Immediately they felt that this time there efforts would be rewarded; the portcullis was moving, and little by little it began to rise, in spite of the friction of the grate against its frame.

Cynthia and Francis redoubled their efforts. The anxious hours they had waited alone seemed to have given them a strength they were previously unaware of.

"There's enough space to slide under," shouted the girl. "Can you brake it?"

"The brake's on," their saviour yelled back.

"Go on," she hissed at Francis.

"And if he takes off the brake?" said the boy, worried and staring at the pointed ends of the vertical bars.

"I don't think he broke his back raising this thing just for the pleasure of watching you get skewered!" replied Cynthia, annoyed. "Go on!"

Francis crouched down and squeezed himself between the points and the floor while his friend kept her grip on the grate, just in case.

He took her place on the other side, thinking that the portcullis was so heavy he wouldn't be able to hold it if the brake came off anyway. But Cynthia wasn't about to be pinned down to the prison flagstones; she slid quickly under the gate and straightened up in the corridor. Their saviour reappeared.

"You were right to start looking for Niki Syeline. His father won't move as long as he hasn't seen him. But Niki isn't here."

Cynthia and Francis had walked over to the man and now could see part of the guard room. Amazed, they saw a second person, equipped like the stranger. And this boy was the one in the photograph which Grigor had given them.

"But it's him!" exclaimed Cynthia.

"Alas, no, that would be too easy," replied the man, smiling. "This young man's name is Marc. Oh, and I'm Carl."

Carl. The girl had the impression that she knew this. But she just couldn't pin it down; where had she met him before?

"The real Niki is aboard a British frigate in the North Sea. We're going to rescue him tonight."

"And bring him here to show to his father?"

"That would be impossible. From the boat they'd contact the castle to announce Niki's escape, and then security measures would be increased here. No, both escapes have to be simultaneous."

"And this ship," Francis asked, still skeptical, "are you just going to board her with cables and grappling-irons, like pirates?"

"Have a bit of faith, Francis. You must have noticed already that we've got a few tricks up our sleeve."

The boy had guessed as much. He asked the obvious question.

"But who are you, anyway?"

Carl became serious and appeared to choose his words carefully.

"We are independent of the great powers. We work for the Secretary General of the United Nations, but without the knowledge of either the Security Council or the General Assembly. We're funded by rich philanthropists, and our technology comes from scientists from the minor powers."

He paused, and then pointed out, "Our existence must remain a secret, and I count on your discretion."

Cynthia, and above all Francis, still didn't know if they should believe Carl. Nevertheless, Carl added, "As far as I'm concerned, you've shown yourselves worthy of trust. The way you tried to free Syeline — that was very courageous and noble."

The girl had a vague feeling that Carl was trying to seduce them with carefully chosen words. But she couldn't imagine him as a traitor. Was he a Soviet agent trying to get his hands on Syeline? But if the Soviets (and the Americans, for that matter) had such formidable lasers and invisibility devices, they wouldn't waste their time with small fry like Syeline.

Apparently certain that both Cynthia and Francis would cooperate with him, the man started telling them of his plan. But all of a sudden he interrupted himself. Putting his hand to his headphone and pressing it to hear better, he concentrated on what he was listening to.

"Someone is about to pay a visit to Trevor MacKinnon. General Dunfries, of NATO. And a truckload of fifteen soldiers."

"How do you know that?" asked Francis with surprise.

"We have observers stationed here and there. Cynthia, can we go without being seen to some place where we can watch the inner courtyard and the entrance to the dungeon?"

The girl led the group to the floor above, cautiously and without noise. Down one long corridor, and then down another, and then finally up a stairway to the second floor in an uninhabited wing, they emerged in an empty, echoing room.

"This is ideal," said Carl, carefully approaching a window.

They could see the whole upper courtyard, the front of the dungeon and part of the lower courtyard. At that moment a limousine drove up and stopped at the foot of the steps leading to the upper courtyard. Trevor MacKinnon went to greet his colleague. Cynthia recognised him.

"That's the man who was angry at grandfather the day we arrived."

"He's bringing him his orders," said Carl.

Carl pointed something at the window that looked like a microphone. After a few adjustments, the conversation between the two generals could be heard from the upper courtyard, even though the window was closed. A tiny instrument, it acted as microphone, filter, amplifier and speaker all together.

"Are you going to blackmail him?" said MacKinnon.

"What I say to Syeline does not concern you, General. You're nothing more than his guardian, here. And not even a very conscientious guardian, by some accounts."

While discussing McSweeny's secret reports, the two men walked over to the dungeon, where the drawbridge was lowered for them. The door opened, they went in, and Carl lost the rest of their conversation.

He called in a low voice into the microphone in his headset. "Phan Vihn, are you picking them up in the dungeon?"

"I'll connect you."

Carl motioned for Cynthia to place her ear near his earphone so that she could hear as well. Marc did the same for Francis, and the four followed the conversation taking place in the dungeon.

"You can't have microphones all over the castle?!" cried Cynthia.

"No, but at each floor in the dungeon. We were there at the same time you were, last night, but we used the tower stairway."

"What about the guards?"

But Andersen had put his finger to his lips. The generals had just arrived at the next to last floor in the dungeon, where Grigor was.

"Well, professor Syeline," began General

Dunfries, "have you thought about our offer?"

"Your demands, more like! I am no freer in my ability to choose than I am to move around."

"We're keeping you here for your protection. You know that the K.G.B. have sent several agents after you."

"I was naïve for so long. Not any more."

"That hardly matters. Will you undertake the research programme we are proposing?"

"You're not asking me to do research, you're asking me to devise an offensive weapon."

Grigor's tone was even, but just from hearing his voice you could tell that he was making a big effort to keep control of himself.

Dunfries, on the other hand, didn't want to waste his time on subtleties. The situation was clear and he didn't have to disguise his intentions any longer.

"We hope that you and your son can be reunited, but your attitude makes that impossible."

"How are you treating him? Do you keep him locked up as well?"

"He has everything he could possibly want. But the K.G.B. is after him as well."

"The only difference between you and the K.G.B. is that they aren't holding Niki."

"Not yet."

There was long silence, and Cynthia imagined Grigor having great difficulty swallowing.

"You won't do that," he replied at long last, his throat sounding very dry. "He wouldn't be of any use to you then."

"That's true. As well, we intend to keep him. But the department has already spent a great deal of money in order to protect you and your boy. This can't go on, and his stay runs the risk of becoming gradually...less luxurious. His food could become a little less refined, less plentiful. You do see, don't you?"

"I see very well," Syeline replied after a painful silence.

Dunfries went on as though Grigor had asked him to. "And then, I am very much afraid that the men who are now keeping him company might begin to take certain liberties with Niki. They might even become distinctly disagreeable."

Again silence. Cynthia clenched her fists as, no doubt, Grigor was also doing up there.

"If that turns out to be too much for him," continued the General, "we might consider transferring him somewhere which could better accommodate a lengthy stay."

"Those animals!" groaned Francis; beside him, Marc nodded bitterly.

"And when do you want my answer?" asked Grigor finally, sounding like a broken man.

"Your answer is already much overdue. Your laboratory awaits you."

"Give me one more day to think it over."

"You have had all the time you need."

"Tomorrow morning, then. Just twelve hours. Be reasonable."

"All right," said Dunfries. "I'll be back for your answer tomorrow morning at eight o'clock. But if it's not the right answer, I am going to be in a very bad mood, and someone will suffer for it."

* * *

The hours in the castle jail had caused Cynthia to lose all sense of time. By the time the interview between Grigor and the generals was over, it was already supper time. MacKinnon started to worry about their disappearance; it was time for her and Francis to reappear.

They took their leave of Carl and Marc, agreeing to a rendezvous that night. The older man gave them an device no bigger than a lighter, but which would enable them to communicate with each other. Then they left, just as mysteriously as they had come, and Cynthia realised with astonishment that they knew the secret passages as well as she did herself.

At the meal, which they ate alone with MacKinnon, the old man was anxious; he seemed to have aged five years since yesterday. The meal was eaten quietly, each person absorbed in his own thoughts. Francis was thinking of all the technology displayed by Carl and

Marc. An incredible idea had occurred to him, an idea he couldn't get out of his head. Yet Marc and he had stood next to each other, shoulder to shoulder, listening to a single earphone, as they followed the conversation between Dunfries and Syeline. Marc had seemed completely human. No extra-terrestrial race could possibly be so similar to the human race; the possibilities for differences were infinite, and the chances of total resemblance were practically nil.

At the end of the meal, MacKinnon spoke to Cynthia and Francis.

"It wasn't a very good idea to put you up so far away, over by the ravine. I have given orders that your belongings be brought to the northern tower where you'll be much happier. At any rate, Gregory is leaving tomorrow; his family has found a private clinic where he'll receive all the care he needs."

Cynthia was speechless, with her mouth literally gaping open. It was so obvious that her grandfather noticed, but he interpreted it wrongly.

"Please, don't be upset that somebody has gone through your things. I would have liked you to pack them up yourself, but you were nowhere to be found."

But that wasn't what was bothering Cynthia. The operation tonight was supposed to begin at the ravine and the subterranean river. Now, Cynthia was willing to bet that the north tower would be under surveillance. They would therefore be unable to reach the underground network.

And Grigor was being taken away tomorrow!

Chapter Sixteen
The Escape

Cynthia had humorously asked her grand-father if guards would be posted at the door of their rooms. The old man had protested; he seemed sincere. But was he still master of his own castle? The north tower had four floors. On the fourth floor, which opened onto a hall-way, there was a soldier discreetly on guard at the end of the corridor. McSweeny must have been behind that.

So the tower was not linked to the net-work of secret passages. But Cynthia and Francis were not short on imagination, and after dis-cussing a plan at some length, they called Marc to change the meeting date.

* * *

James, one of the second floor guards, found the time long leaning against the wall of the darkened corridor, watching a closed door. He wasn't a stranger to this kind of work, but it was the first time he had worked in such a vast and complex structure — with the task of keeping an eye on two overly curious adolescents.

Suddenly the door some distance away opened. James whispered to his buddy sitting in a room nearby:

"They're coming out!"

But what odd behaviour. Each of them was holding a candlestick, behaving like actors or mime artists playing the role of conspirators. They were walking on tiptoe, lifting their knees high, turning their heads in fits and starts. They seemed to be having a great time, trying to keep from laughing, whispering so loudly that James could hear them in spite of the distance. The guard thought they were playing pranks on MacKinnon, the grandfather.

James hurried, followed by his companion, Allan. They couldn't see the youngsters because of the right-angle turn in the hallway. At the turn, James noticed the boy, still acting like a comedian, disappearing around a turn in the corridor The soldiers quickened their pace; this castle had so many staircases and halls that it was easy to lose track of someone. And indeed, that is what happened. After the turn in the corridor which skirted the chapel's choir-loft, there were a few steps going up, and then another turn. A door was slightly open leading into a dimly lit room; Cynthia and Francis were not to be seen.

They must be in there, thought the soldier, but he didn't hear their voices. The only movement was the flickering of the candle flame, so he slowed down. After pausing a moment, James decided to carefully open the door; the room was empty. Two lit candlesticks stood on the buffet.

"Hell!"

Further on, the corridor divided again, and one had to choose between a spiral staircase servicing this side of the castle, an a corridor with a number of steps going down and then another turn. Where had they gone, those two pranksters?

"Look," breathed Allan.

Stained glass windows were set into the inner wall, and light was filtering through them from behind.

"In the chapel! Go keep an eye on the other door, but don't go in."

James hurried toward one of the doors that was just slightly open. the vast hall was in total darkness and appeared deserted. He pushed the door open and went in. Two candelabra with five branches were burning on the altar; that explained the light in the stained glass windows. But who had just lit them?

James came forward a few steps and slowly turned his head. The silence was total. Back behind the last pew, a bluish glow seemed to appear gradually. James felt shivers run down his spine. He and the other soldiers had only been in the castle a few hours and already ghost stories abounded. Was the chapel haunted?

The soldier sought out his buddy and together they made their way toward the back of the room, each by a different aisle. James was particularly anxious; he had seen that cold, blue light appear out of nowhere.

Unless the two pranksters were hiding behind the pews?

The soldiers got to the back of the room. There was no one. Just a few blue vigil lights, set on the flagstones, throwing a soft glow over the stillness of the chapel.

* * *

Two floors below, in the immense burial crypt where almost all the MacKinnons were laid to rest, Marc Alix became visible again. That is, he would have become visible if there had been any light. With his mini-flashlight, he gave the appropriate signal.

A glow appeared in the depths of the crypt; two silhouettes were visible. Marc went to meet them.

"Our guards?" asked Cynthia in a subdued voice.

"They're asking themselves if a soldier should believe in ghosts."

Between two massive tombs, the entrance to a secret stairway had already been opened. They entered, Cynthia closing the panel noiselessly behind them. All the doors and traps had been lubricated during the evening by Carl and his accomplices.

"Bad news," announced Marc, now that they were safely in. "The soldiers sent by General Dunfries are not only here to keep an eye on you two; there are soldiers in the dungeon as well, and probably in the adjoining rooms. Do you think McSweeny has any insight into your plans?"

"Gee...the chauffeur may have found out about our expeditions into the ravine. He would have told McSweeny. But I'm the only one who knows the underground passages."

"McSweeny mustn't be underestimated. He would certainly have guessed that underground passages *existed.* And Syeline has asked for a delay. Why, they would have asked themselves? Because Syeline hopes to escape."

He paused. Cynthia noticed how tense he was and figured that he must have good reason to be worried.

"I have more bad news," he continued. "Reinforcements have just been sent to this area. One platoon has taken up position in the ravine, and another close to the village. They have surrounded the little house that was our base of operations. There's been too much coming and going. The army must have planted a spy in the village who caught on to it. We've underestimated the security measures with regard to Syeline: Very discreet, but very much there."

"It's a bust," gasped Francis, floored.

"Not necessarily. They still have to find the underground passages. My men are watching their movements carefully."

"Do we still have time to free Grigor?"

"If we move quickly."

They went down the secret staircase, past the lowest dungeon cellars, already occupied by the enemy. At the foot of the vertical shaft, everything was quiet and silent. They started up.

Marc had tuned his receiver on the microphones hidden on each floor of the dungeon. When the three reached the first floor, Marc Stopped.

"Your escapade has been discovered," he said in a hushed voice, the receiver pressed against his ear. "McSweeny and Dunfries have come to see if Syeline is still imprisoned."

As he reported what he was hearing, Marc slid through the first floor trap. He opened it slowly. McSweeny could be heard interrogating the guard stationed at the drawbridge and door.

Marc removed a small cylindrical object from his belt and threw it across the floor of the guard room. He closed the trap door again; the muffled sound of an explosion could scarcely be heard.

"A soporific gas," he explained in a low

voice. "Let's go on."

They went up as fast as they could, given the condition of the carved rungs. The dungeon seemed higher than ever before.

At the top, Marc eased himself under the trap door first, and opened it slightly. Beyond the piece of furniture, he saw that a soft light filtered through the room. Along with Syeline, there were two guards seated on chairs — they didn't appear to be on the verge of falling asleep, of allowing their prisoner to escape.

Marc drew a pistol from his belt, adjusted the barrel extension. He'd been trained at Argus, but the regional headquarters; and again a little while ago, but not enough as far as he was concerned. He took aim at the closest leg. There was the barely audible hiss of compressed air. It struck the guard in the calf, and already a lightning-quick anaesthetic was circulating in his blood. Body heat would cause the dart to dissolve.

The other guard saw the first one jump; then he saw him waver. Worried, he got up from his chair.

"What's the...?"

In the thigh. The guard brought his had up to the site of the injection, fell to his knees and collapsed. Syeline rushed over to the trap door. Marc, invisible under the dresser, handed him a mini-grenade.

"Throw that onto the stairs, quick, and close the door."

But already, a third guard came into the room. He must have been sitting close by in the stairway. Marc, putting all subtlety aside, aimed for the chest. The man was struck down.

Syeline threw the grenade, and holding his breath, rushed to close the door. Under the trap door, Marc went back down the chimney to leave room for his companions.

Grigor had had the foresight to empty the drawers of the dresser to lighten it, and had removed the vase.

"Is Niki with you?"

"Yes, come down, quickly."

The hardest thing to do was to put the dresser back in its place, but it had to be done. Finally, with three pairs of arms, they managed to do it.

"Where is Niki?" asked the worried Syeline.

"Lower down," answered Cynthia. "We didn't want to crowd the passageway."

As planned, she beamed her flashlight down to where Marc, three floors down, was looking up at them. At this distance, and with this amount of light, Grigor was convinced.

"My son," he shouted in Russian, but Cynthia shushed him in an authoritative tone.

"This chimney is very resonant," she whispered.

So Marc was exempted from answering the Soviet's call, which would probably have given him away.

136

Francis led the way; shielding the father from the phony son was part of their strategy.

"The escape will be discovered soon," explained the young girl in a hushed voice. "Hugging you son will have to be put off till later."

She hated herself for being so brusque with Grigor, most of all for deceiving him. But it was for his own good, and this was no time for scruples.

They finally reached the base of the chimney. Passing each floor, Marc had listened to the microphones on each level. On the cellar levels, he noticed there was a commotion: coughing, muffled calls. The grenade thrown on the first floor had alerted them.

At the stairway, Marc did not stop but continued on to the well, undertaking the spiral descent to the underground lake. Grigor Syeline was alarmed, but above all astonished.

"Couldn't he wait for me? He'll get lost!"

"We had time to show him the passageways; he knows the way. We told him how hurried we'd be."

In the well, the fugitive could see his son in the spiral staircase, four or five turns lower. "Niki" saw him too, and waved to him from a distance; Syeline thought he recognised him. Convinced that his son was being detained here in the castle, it never occurred to him that it could be someone resembling his son. The poor lighting, the hurriedness, were enough for him not to notice the dissimilarity between Marc and the real Niki.

"Not a word," uttered Cynthia to the parental fugitive. "We're in a well and the guards are right above us."

In fact, there was a little circle of light at the top: the cellars were lit. *As long as nobody thinks to look in the well,* Cynthia thought. But her hopes were soon shattered. There were silhouetted shapes up there, busying themselves. Maybe they were trying to lower a soldier with a rope and winch to see if there was a way of escape in the well. Cynthia flicked off her flashlight; Francis' would be enough for all three.

Further down, Marc had other reasons to be alarmed. Phan Vihn, from the cottage cellar, had just sent a message that soldiers had invaded the cottage and were entering the underground river tunnel, having just discovered the entrance a few minutes before. They must have heard about the escape and were trying to abort it.

* * *

The cavern at the end of the well was not dark. A series of lights extended from the foot of the stairway, along the ledge, as far as the cave which opened onto the sea. Lights even shone in the water. Kati Vogel was waiting impatiently for the fugitives and looking discouragingly at the water churning in the cave. Normally at low tide, they should have been able to to come out of the cave without getting their feet wet and get right into the boat anchored outside. When they were a certain distance from the cliff, the fugitives were to be met by an Argus submarine which had moved into the firth earlier that evening. But the sea was rough, with each wave almost reaching the ceiling of the passageway before breaking noisily in the cave.

Marc was the first to reach the cavern. Kati hurried to meet him, but she didn't need to explain the situation to him. The young man could see the problem at a glance.

"We'll never get through. Even if we swim."

Oxygen bottles, respirators and flippers were ready in case the escape was delayed or had to be accomplished at high tide; the equipment was lined up along the rock ledge. Just below, the water rose rhythmically, full of whorls forming white foam, while the underwater light gave a greenish hue to the agitated waters.

The opershuttle called. "The rain should stop and the wind should die down. But the sea needs more time to settle down. We'll have to wait an hour before going through; especially with inexperienced divers."

"But we don't have an hour; the troops are advancing through the underground passages."

Marc took the headpiece that Kati handed him; it was light and equipped with a communications system and an infrared visor.

"Phan?" he whispered into the speaker. "Phan Vihn?"

"The situation is under control," answered the Erymean. "The equipment in the cottage cellar disintegrated correctly. The heat caused by the fusion slowed the soldiers down. I'm almost at the fork at the underground river. The other troops are still far away; I can hardly see the glow from their lights."

Cynthia, Francis and Grigor had just arrived at the cavern, a few moments earlier. And when the Soviet saw the young man acting as chief of operations, most of all speaking a strange language, he knew that it was not his son. He thrust himself at him.

"Where is Niki? This is a trick! A trap!"

"Marc felt the wave of emotion crashing up against him: fear, anger, despair. Fear for his son who was still a prisoner, anger at having been deceived, despair at having fallen once again into the hands of kidnappers In one flashing moment, the young man saw his uncle, Horace Guillon, who also had been caught in the army's dragnet, who had been cheated and used and driven to despair. And he saw himself, Marc, caught up in events beyond his control, a victim of blind and cruel forces, as was Niki of late.

He took Grigor's hand in his and pressed it compassionately. He spoke to him in faltering Russian, a language he had learned too hastily.

"At this very moment, Niki's escape is underway; he was held on a British ship. The escapes had to be executed simultaneously, you must understand. I had to lie so that you'd agree to escape tonight. Here..."

Despite the urgency of the moment, Marc made a spontaneous gesture: from Kati's belt, he removed an instrument equipped with a mini-screen for long-distance communications.

"Opershuttle Syeline-Scott," he called. "Are you in touch with Syeline-Orkneys?"

"Yes, the raid is in progress. It doesn't seem to be easy from what I can gather. I don't think there's time for a conversation."

Marc made a gesture of impatience, almost of despair. He faced Grigor again, and stuttered nervously in Russian.

"Listen. In a few minutes, I promise you, in a few minutes you'll see Niki on this little screen; you'll be able to speak to him. Do you understand?"

Syeline looked at him, almost assuaged. He could see by Marc's gestures and words that he was sincere. Such spontaneity could not have been feigned, he thought, except by the greatest of actors. Or was Grigor being naïve once again?

"I understand what you're saying," he answered in English. "I choose to believe you. For the time being."

141

Marc sighed with relief, but soon he was cut short by Cynthia. "Where do we go now?"

"We have to climb back up, we've got no choice. We'll get picked up on the dungeon's terrace or on a curtain wall."

"Not again!" exclaimed Francis, who already felt weak in the knees.

"Kati," ordered Marc, you throw the diving gear in the water. With a bit of luck it'll never be found. Then you turn off the lights. With Phan, you'll hold the rear. Grenades if needed."

So the fugitives set off again up the stairs, undertaking the ascent of the well, keeping the light of their lamps to the ground so as not to be spotted from up above.

To no avail: up there, they glimpsed shining dots, the soldiers' flashlights. The military had found out that a secret passage led to the well, and they were looking for a way to reach it from the dungeon's cellars. As the entrance to that secret passage had not yet been found, they were descending inside the well with ropes, down to the place where the staircase began.

The fugitives were surrounded.

Chapter Seventeen
Operation Syeline-Orkneys

One by one the floodlights lit up on the forward deck of the frigate Defiant, making a shimmering mist out of the rain. Between the Orkneys and the Shetlands, the storm had subsided at the beginning of the evening, but the sea was still rough.

On the bridge, Captain Burridge complained bitterly about the Admiralty, which had authorised the transfer of the Syeline boy in the middle of a storm. One helicopter lost, one ship damaged, injuries and probably some casualties, that's what was at stake. And all because of a matter which, from the beginning, was unsound. Who was this Russian boy; why were they guarding him; and above all, why was he being urgently called back to Scotland in the middle of the night?

Burridge approached the bay window which was being swept by powerful wipers, and put on a headset by which he could communicate with his first officer on the forward deck. There Jenkins, who was responsible for the young Soviet, appeared in a hatchway. The boy was with him, a suitcase in his hand, his face pale under the hood of his oilskins.

"Front starboard," signalled an officer. "Helicopter lights."

Burridge located it, its coloured lights barely visible, its strobe lighting up a little halo of rain with each flash. Its landing lights suddenly came on.

"Can you see it?" he asked into his microphone.

"And hear it," responded his first officer on the bridge.

They could hear it over the roar of the ocean, at that distance? Burridge looked on attentively. He couldn't even see the silhouette of the aircraft, especially now the lights were on. It was suspended up there, now almost directly in front, seemingly hesitant to land. And Burridge understood why; in the rough sea, the bridge of the Defiant was rocking to and fro, up to an angle of ten degrees. Luckily the wind was light, but there were gusts which he could see clearly in the rain illuminated by the floodlights.

"This is ridiculous," the captain suddenly burst out. "Get me the pilot of this chopper..."

Several flashes in rapid succession interrupted him. He saw a pink smoke spreading out over the forward deck, and then in front of the bay window of the bridge itself. Then he had a sickly sweet odour in his throat. That smoke...

"Isolate the bridge!"

The air vents were closed, the independent air-supply began to ventilate the room, as it would during an attack or a fire. But it was a bit late; the captain and his officers began to stagger, seized by a sudden sleepiness. Burridge fell to his knees, catching hold of the frame of the bay window. Only his head showed through the window. He could see, through the smoke which was already dissipating, the silhouettes of the emergency team stretched out on the bridge. Then the floodlights dimmed and went out. All that remained was the light from the helicopter, which seemed to dance in the captain's vertigo, just before he too lost consciousness.

* * *

The helicopter, of course, was nothing of the kind, any more than the coded message to the Defiant had been authentic. It was an opershuttle, one of the shuttles specially equipped for Operations, it had used lights, a searchlight and a high-powered speaker system to simulate the sound of the helicopter rotors.

Meanwhile, a second opershuttle, this one invisible because of its optic deflector and anti-radar screen, approached and launched with great precision a volley of soporific grenades, some of which had been aimed to explode directly in front of the ship's air vents. Of course, where there is wind to disperse the sleep-inducing gas, you can only count on several minutes of inertia.

Having disabled the ship's lighting system, the opershuttle began to land. The landing was done by automatic pilot which, along with the antigrav and altivers, was helped by verniers, little lateral rockets, so that it could react in a millisecond to the gusts of wind and the slower pitching of the ship.

At the Norwegian base, Carl Andersen had met up with Tram Phong, who three years earlier had helped him rescue Marc Alix. This night, she was leading a crack commando team equipped with gas masks, communication headsets and infrared visors. If all went well, they could complete the operation and be back in the opershuttle in under a minute.

There was sudden jolt: the front shock absorbers had banged against the bridge. The rear ones then touched down more gently. For a second, the craft skidded on the wet surface, and then came to a halt. The rear door opened, a step-ladder sprang down, and the Argus agents dashed into the rain, into the darkness. But the night was not dark for them; it was full of confused objects glowing different tones of green. The bodies stretched out on the bridge were a luminous jade green.

Unlike his comrades, Carl wasn't armed. Followed by another agent, he ran to the hatchway where Niki Syeline had been located before the landing. Fortunately, because of the angle of the ship when the grenades had exploded, Niki hadn't fallen down the staircase leading to the lower bridges.

Carl slipped, due to the pitching of the vessel, and fell on his side, but didn't hurt himself. Jenkins had collapsed on top of Niki; Carl heaved his body aside. He pressed an oxygen mask onto the boy's face, and strapped it in place.

"Take his legs," he shouted to the comrade who had followed him.

Together, struggling to keep their balance, they carried the unconscious body to the shuttle, where the rest of the commando unit was already beginning to retreat. The ladder and door were highlighted by infrared lamps which seemed like so many white points through Carl's visor. He handed Niki to a doctor who had stayed on the ship, and then climbed up himself. Already, Tram Phong had sounded the retreat.

"Back on board!"

Quickly, but in impeccable order in spite of the sloping deck, the commando team regained the ship. Carl was already strapped into the copilot's seat.

"Full house!" shouted Tram Phong, signalling that everyone was on board.

The pilot was waiting for the moment when the ship was as close to horizontal as possible; when that happened he took off. At that instant, the emergency floodlights lit up on the front bridge of the ship...

* * *

Captain Burridge was only unconscious
for a short time. But someone just behind him,
an officer, had awakened up even more quickly
and had put on the emergency lighting system.
Picking himself up with great difficulty, Burridge tried to clear his head and figure out what
had happened to him. In the bluish light, the
forward deck seemed empty. There was nothing except a sort of turbulence that was slowly
rising, with occasionally a sudden glare he
couldn't make out, and puffs of steam under the
rain. And then the floodlights went out again,
one by one, before the captain had really been
able to see anything precise.

Had it been a gust, a little whirlwind? Was
it just the floodlights blinking as they tried to
relight themselves? Through the rain, it was
impossible to say. Burridge was even having
difficulty remembering why the floodlights were
supposed to be on on the forward deck.

During the hastily convened inquiry
which Burridge and lieutenant Jenkins con-
ducted during the next hour, no one would
remember anything. There were just odds and
ends; some thought a helicopter might have
been trying to land, others recalled dimly the
floodlights going out. No one remembered how
he had lost consciousness. The sleeping-gas
also had the effect of erasing all memory of
those last moments of consciousness.

No one would ever know how Niki
Syeline had disappeared.

148

* * *

The two opershuttles streaked towards the Norwegian regional base, their pilots worrying little about the storm. Carl leaned back in his seat and turned to ask, "How is he?"

The doctor had seated Niki on a chair which he had tilted back. He had connected his mask to a supply of pure oxygen, the best antidote for sleeping gas. The boy was already beginning to show some signs of life.

"He's a little pale, a little thin," said the doctor. "I think he must have been seasick and eaten little in the last few days. Otherwise, there's no sign that he was treated badly."

Carl turned back to the controls, and started asking about the other operation.

"Opershuttle Syeline-Scott, how far have they gotten?"

"It's not good. They were unable to escape through the marine cavern. The troop has invaded the tunnels and is converging on the bottom of the well. Another platoon is going into the well from the dungeon. Marc Alix and his group are caught between them."

Carl felt a wave of anguish and despair sweep over him. *I should never have left him,* he thought, *it was too risky.* He turned towards the pilot.

"Change direction. We're going to Scotland."

Chapter Eighteen
The Dragon's Lair

"Cynthia," asked Marc, "are we far from that side gallery that leads to the cliff?"

"The soldiers will reach it before we do."

"Masks, everybody."

Marc, and Kati who had rejoined the group, distributed the mask-respirators which had filters to neutralise soporific gas.

Up above, the soldiers had found the hidden trap door which opened onto the steps leading to the well. Some ten soldiers had gone into the well and were making their way down the spiral staircase.

The young man took a grenade from his cartridge belt: it was not much bigger than a roll of 35mm film. He inserted it into the compressed air barrel of his grenade launcher. He did not need his infrared visor; the light from the soldiers' torches was sufficient. He chose a grenade whose gas was lighter than air, and he set it to go off in one second.

"Is it the gas that puts them to sleep?" asked Francis. "The soldiers will fall into the well."

"They'll be conscious for five to six seconds, long enough to control where they fall. In any case, I have no choice."

He had no choice, but he hoped with all his heart that there would be no accidents. Pof! The grenade-launcher pistol jolted his hand. One second later, a pink glow exploded up above, generating a cloud of spreading smoke.

"Let's go up!" ordered Marc. "As fast as possible without risking anything."

Up above, worried and astonished exclamations echoed through the air, but as yet, there was no coughing. The grenade had not exploded high enough. And the gas, which would normally rise in a stable atmosphere, was being pulled downward by the air drafts which were always flowing in the wells. It was spreading towards the bottom as well as at the top.

Marc picked up Phan Vihn's voice on his receiver.

"The two platoons which invaded the tunnels are stopped some distance from the cavern: I exploded some grenades at the tunnel's exit."

"Where are you now?"

"I'm about to climb up the well."

The cloud of smoke has thinned. The soldiers' electric torches no longer threw any light. But Marc was careful. He pulled down his infra-red visor, turned the close-up knob. He inspected the walls of the well, where the recessed staircase turned in spirals like the threads of a screw.

He wasn't mistaken. He noticed a head with a beret, a face with eyes wide open, looking down.

Marc set another grenade at one second and inserted it into the barrel of his pistol. This time, the delay should be enough; they weren't as far away. Inching forward again on the edge of the abyss, he extended his arm upward and fired.

The sound of coughing followed the spreading cloud of smoke. Then Marc saw a body, arms crossed, somersaulting like a trapeze artist through space, pierce through the gas cloud and fall into the well.

The young man fell back, horrified. He heard a thud, boots hitting against the rock face, and he saw the body as it passed, a phantom in the green darkness of his visor. The body bounced two or three more times against the rock face or the ridges of the steps, and the metallic clanging of his weapon falling with him resounded into the distance, as the body splashed into the water.

Shattered, Marc could not move for a moment. This should not have happened. The operation was supposed to unfold without violence, cleanly, with hardly anyone knowing about it. But everything was amiss almost from the beginning. Marc could do nothing but react to the enemy, running from one place to another like a cornered rat.

"Marc!" called Phin Vihn into his receiver. "Who fell?"

He didn't answer immediately, being still obsessed with the image of the soldier who, at this very minute, was drowning in the icy water, probably half-conscious.

"Marc! Who fell?"

"We're all here," he answered in a hoarse voice.

Up above, Kati Vogel, reassured as well, was leading the escape of the Earthlings. At the level of the gas cloud, she noticed an opening in the rock face. Through her infra-red visor, the rock face was a deeper shade of green. She stopped and immediately noticed that there was a lighter-coloured shape in the horizontal tunnel: the warm colour of a body. Quickly, she aimed with her dart pistol. That was a soldier there. Leading the way, the two grenades must have missed him, but not completely. He was slumped over, leaning against the rock face, and wavering. He heard the group coming and raised his gun.

An anaesthetic dart struck him down. His weapon fell to the ground and fired off with a deafening sound, the bullet ricocheting off the rocks but not hitting anyone. Down below, the detonation and frightened exclamations that followed wakened Marc from his stupor. He darted out, calling into his microphone, "Kati! Anyone hurt?"

"No one."

This horizontal tunnel, several metres below the castle's cellars, led to a natural grotto in the cliff. Very narrow, hardly ever used, it was really a simple break in the rock. It was the fugitive's last exit, the last refuge if things went wrong.

A few steps into the gallery, however, Grigor Syeline stopped Cynthia:

"That's enough. I trusted you, Cynthia and Francis, because you were children. But you are not the ones who organised this escape. What proof do I have that I'm not giving myself up to some new tyrant?"

Marc walked past Francis, toward Syeline removing his video communicator.

"Opershuttle Syeline-Scott," he called.

"All is well?"

"No. Put me in touch with Syeline-Orcades."

"Over."

"Carl? Is the boy with you?"

"Yes, he's coming around. But you? What's happening?"

"It can wait. Let Niki come on the screen; his father wants to speak to him."

The picture of the boy appeared on the mini-screen, perfectly clear.

"Here, have a few words with him," said Marc handing the instrument over to Grigor. "Quietly, if you don't mind."

He moved away, and left the Soviet to express his joy more freely. Marc said to Kati: "Run over to the grotto and guide the opershuttle."

Back in the well, he greeted Phan Vihn: "Tired?"

"I'll be all right."

All the Argus spies were athletes in peak physical condition.

"Do you mind holding up the rear? In a minute, throw a grenade straight ahead on the rock face of the well. That should block any access to the tunnel. Then run toward us."

"Everything will be all right," she told him, and she squeezed his arm to give him courage.

She had been involved in these kinds of missions when Marc was still in grammar school.

The young man returned to the three Earthlings.

"Last phase, we hope," he called out. "Grigor, you can keep this toy, but start walking. And quickly."

Guided by the lights from Cynthia and Francis' flashlights, they walked through the passageway, which was not very long. The tunnel grew larger, becoming a natural grotto, more high than wide, its floor sloping and uneven. From the outside, even in the full light of day, it looked like a deep crevice.

"What could this cave have been used for?" asked Francis, staying cautiously away from the edge.

"Legend has it that it was a lair of the notorious dragon. Its nest, if you prefer. He fled from here to terrorise the region."

155

"No, but seriously?"

"I've no idea. The fissure did exist, and they found it when they dug the well."

After so much time spent underground, the sea air filled them with hope. At least that's how it was for Marc and Kati; the Earthlings didn't realise that this cave opening at mid-cliff could serve as a exit. From top to bottom, only a well-equipped mountain-climber could climb the cliff. Sixty metres below, the waves, subsiding somewhat, crashed noisily against the rocks. It was a dark, totally overcast night, and the sea foam was barely visible. Were it not for the breeze and the sound of the sea, one could not have told that they were in the open air.

"Grigor," asked Marc, "did your son tell you where he was?"

"A kind of small aircraft," he said, "but he had never seen anything quite like it."

"Well, it'll be the same for you."

He pulled down his infra-red visor. Even without an optical deflector, the opershuttle was invisible in the dark. Now he saw it, very close by already, oscillating gently in the calm breeze. Held aloft by its own antigravs, it manoeuvred slowly, backing up using the thrust of its verniers.

"Phan, throw the grenade and come," shouted Marc through the microphone.

"I see something," exclaimed Cynthia.

She had noticed, in front of the cave, the light jet of the little rockets, silhouetting the dark mass of the opershuttle.

"But it's...What is it?...We don't hear anything."

In a quieter environment, she would have heard a hum and the hissing sounds of the verniers. But tonight, this silent apparition must have been frightening, a mass with rounded edges, short fins, a vertical aileron, and now, jets whose hot breath could be felt in the depths of the cave.

The rear of the opershuttle was in the cave, but not far in because of its wings, which were partially retracted. The shock absorbers extended slowly, looking for a place to touch down on the uneven ground. They extended fully before setting down. The hatch opened by sliding laterally, revealing the rose-coloured lighting of the cabin. Powerful lights over the door illuminated the ramp, which opened out fully without reaching the sloping ground of the cave.

It's a UFO, Francis thought, and there was no longer any doubt in his mind that these mysterious rescuers were extra-terrestrial beings. Then why did they look so completely human? And the more crucial question: were they to be trusted and followed into their craft? What was known of their real intentions? Weren't they known to have abducted Earthlings before?

"We'll have to perform some acrobatics," announced Marc. "Kati will show you."

Going down among the rough rocks, Kati almost went to the edge of the cliff before she could climb onto the first step of the ramp. Her silhouette appeared illuminated against the doorway of the hatch. Cynthia followed, then Grigor, who still hadn't turned off the mini-screen of the communicator.

Phan Vihn came running into the cave, perfectly calm.

"Down below, they had started to come up but the grenade stopped them."

Francis didn't want to go on. One false step and he would tumble down to the cliff and from there into the sea. He could see the void, a space of perfect blackness between the underside of the craft and the last rocks on the slope. Marc came up to him.

"Is it vertigo?"

The boy nodded. But his fear wasn't due to vertigo.

"Follow me."

And Marc, who was scarcely any braver when it came to heights, went first, showing the young Earthling the best places to put his feet, and where to grab on with his hands. From the last rocky projection to the ladder, there was a distance of about one meter. Marc climbed up onto the metal steps and extended his hand to the boy.

"There you go. It wasn't that bad."

But Francis didn't breathe easily until he was through the hatchway. There, something else took his breath away, just as it had done to Cynthia and Grigor. One thing was for sure — these people weren't Earthlings.

Phan Vihn got in last, the ladder was retracted and the door closed. The opershuttle moved away from the cliff and lifted off gently so as not to attract any attention.

Marc turned to face the many questions his fugitives had for him.

Chapter Nineteen
Return to Erymede

Cynthia was confused. There had been so many things happening and so many surprises that she'd forgotten a little how she felt about Grigor. And then, seeing him overflowing with joy, full of anxious care as the picture of his son appeared on the screen, and then crying openly when he had seen him in person and was able to kiss him... To see all this made Cynthia understand that Grigor had a son, and that his son was to him the dearest thing in the world. In the same instant, she realised that Grigor probably didn't have much room in his heart for another love. In any case, he probably didn't have room for the all-engrossing and capricious love of an eighteen year old girl. Besides, this new Grigor was not at all the Gregory that her imagination had blown out of proportion, starting with the image of a young and visionary poet held prisoner up in a tower.

She even felt a little stupid to have been carried off that way on the basis of a few brief visions and encounters. But now another person had captured her attention. The younger of their two saviours, the one who had led the wild flight through the castle tunnels. Marc. He was in one of the shuttles and she could see him through the open door, in the pink lighting of the cabin. He looked a little absent, a little tragic, like those who have escaped mortal danger. He wasn't talking, he was grim, and that made him look even more lovely; only eighteen or nineteen, but already he had a certain maturity to his appearance. And in his blue-grey eyes lay the attraction of the unknown.

* * *

What was haunting Marc and making him so sombre was the death of the soldier, caused by the grenade he had thrown. Phan Vihn, who had been nearer to the underground lake, had told him that she had neither seen nor heard any sort of splashing after his plunge, nothing to indicate that the man had regained the surface and swum away. The only thing she could tell Marc, by way of consolation, was that the soldier could not have been conscious of his drowning, perhaps not even of his fall.

"If he fell, it was because of the gas which was freed right beside him as he was breathing; one concentrated puff and he would have been unconscious even before he fell. He didn't suffer, he didn't even have time to feel afraid."

This made Marc feel a little better, but not entirely; after all, he had been the one to throw the grenade.

"You didn't have any choice," Carl repeated to him. "In sending them to sleep, you avoided something much worse. There could have shooting, people wounded and even killed, especially in your group. You didn't ask for any of this."

"Neither did that poor soldier."

"I know that. He wasn't the one who locked up Syeline and tormented his son. But he probably did choose to be a soldier, and he would have been exposed to much worse if he'd been sent to Ireland."

"That doesn't justify anything."

"Nothing justifies death. It just is. It's not something you deserve, it's just something that happens. To everybody. You were just the instrument, you didn't decide it should happen. Any more than the grenade, or the well, or the underground lake, or his commander."

"Erymean morals," Marc commented bitterly.

"Erymean philosophy. Without it we couldn't play the part we do."

That at least was true. Without the grenades, Marc and his companions wouldn't have been able to save Grigor and Niki. They couldn't have saved them from anguish, perhaps from torture, and as a result preserved the world, at least for a couple of years, from a weapon of dreadful power.

That too relieved Marc's remorse. Time, even if it took years, would help him bear the rest.

* * *

The three opershuttles were on a beach, on the west coast of the Firth of Moray. The country was deserted and the coast battered with wind and waves. On the other side of the Firth, of the estuary, the MacKinnon castle was of course invisible. Even lit up as it was on this night of turmoil, it would have been invisible except during clear weather.

The time had come to make decisions. The Erymeans had explained where they really came from and why they had saved the Syelines. The technology they had deployed that night was sufficient proof to the Earthlings that Erymede existed.

They had offered to either bring Grigor and Niki back to Erymede or to establish them in a country far from Great Britain and the Soviet Union. They could begin life again in New Zealand or Australia; they would be furnished with all the documents necessary to create a new identity, since Argus had the best counter-feiters in existence.

They also offered Cynthia and Francis the choice of leaving for Erymede or going back to the castle; if to the castle, they would tie them up and leave them in some remote corner to make it look like that had had nothing to do with the escape, but had been surprised and neutral-ised by the kidnappers.

All four, if they chose not to come to Erymede, would have to undergo amnesiac treatment — a drug which would erase the memory either of the last few hours or the last few days, depending on the dose. And the Erymeans would suggest alternative memories to fill up whatever time period was wiped out. These false memories would be absolutely true for them, and would fool even a lie-detector. That was what Carl had done for Cynthia a year before, after she had willingly allowed him to visit the underground network at the castle. She had only retained a vague remembrance of his face, his name.

The final reunion took place in the cabin of an opershuttle, filled with noise of the sea because the door to the craft had been left open. There was little time in which to reflect; a decision had to be made.

The Earthlings chose earth.

Grigor Syeline, perhaps not totally convinced, decided upon Auckland in New Zealand.

"At any rate," he explained, "I'm too old to adapt to a society so radically different as that of Erymede must be."

Niki hesitated, but because he had suffered so much during the years of separation from his father, he chose to follow him to Auckland.

The decision wasn't easy for anyone. Cynthia wanted very much to follow Marc, whom she found so fascinating, back to his planet. But she realised as well that once again she had become impassioned very quickly, and that her feelings might well subside abruptly as well, just as they had done for Grigor. Would they then let her return to Earth to be with Francis?

"I think I'll stay," she finally decided. "There are many things I can do here, on Earth. I can become a member of Amnesty International, for instance, or find other ways to stop scientists from being kidnapped and forced to work against their will. And I can try to stop governments from holding children hostage in order to coerce their parents."

She was thinking of Chile and other similar countries, about which horror stories were sometimes told.

Francis, for his part, was not convinced that a mere Earthling could ever change either the mentality or behaviour of other Earthlings. Erymede attracted him a lot, just as it had Marc, but then Marc hadn't had a choice. Francis was a little afraid of the unknown. And, above all, he still had many attachments on Earth. He had his family, his younger brothers, Cynthia, his friends. There were too many ties to break them all at once.

"You couldn't..." He hesitated briefly. "You couldn't come back and offer me this choice in five years? I think I'd be more able to make a mature decision then."

Carl and Marc looked at each other. For Carl, it was out of the question; Argus only ever recruited exceptional Earthlings, or welcomed refugees in exceptional circumstances like Marc's had been. But to grant such a favour... Marc was tempted to say yes. Had he remained an Earthling, he and Francis might well have been friends. Marc could very well have been in the same situation as Francis, and he would have appreciated the time to think things over.

"We'll try," he said impulsively. "We can't promise anything, but we'll try."

Stunned, Carl didn't dare contradict him in front of Francis.

"In any case," he said, "we'll have to erase all your memories of the last few hours. We can't exempt you from that."

He'll forget that Erymede exists, thought Carl, *and he won't ever regret having declined our offer.*

When they were alone, away from the Earthlings, Carl reproached his friend.

"That was pretty irresponsible, what you promised Francis. Recruitment will not be tied down by this."

"I will be," said Marc. "I trade a good deed for a bad one."

"You're thinking of that soldier?"

"If I could do some Earthling a favour... It wouldn't bring back that poor soldier, but my conscience..."

Carl didn't pursue the matter.

166

* * *

Several days later, Marc was readying himself to get back to Erymede. But one last thing was worrying him, and he went, with Carl, to the main Argus Control room. They were directed to one of the officers in charge of monitoring the outcome of the Syeline affair. One of Argus's spy satellites had been put in a geo-stationary orbit above Scotland.

"There was army deployment the day after the escape. It was under the pretext of manoeuvrers. In fact, they explored the whole promontory, the slopes, the ravine, the cliffs, the wooded areas. They probably searched every meter of the underground caverns and the castle. The next day they left, because the press was starting to pay attention. Also, remember that general MacKinnon has friends at the defence department. Apparently, they have stopped trying to find the fugitives; they've handed the whole thing over to counter-espionage."

"What I want to know," said Marc, "is what happened to Cynthia and Francis. Were they suspected, or did the army leave them alone?"

The night of the escape, near dawn, the opershuttle Syeline-Scott had dropped Cynthia and Francis on the curtain wall near the chapel, using a diversion which almost emptied the castle of soldiers. Carl and Kati Vogel had bound and gagged them, and had left them half-conscious in the belfry, within the reach of the bells so that they could call for help when they woke up.

"I think they have returned to their normal lives," said the officer. "I asked a shuttle which was returning to the Norwegian base to detour via the MacKinnon castle and take pictures."

As he spoke, the office called up an aerial photograph of the stony landscape of the promontory, in front of the castle. Two horsemen could be seen descending the road which ran along the cliff to the bridge.

"Close-up?" asked Carl.

When the image was enlarged, it was possible to recognise the two young riders; Cynthia's reddish blond mop, and Francis's brown mane, almost as long. They appeared content.

"With general MacKinnon to protect them," Carl said, "they won't have anything to fear from anyone who accuses them. Especially because Cynthia is the daughter of a diplomat."

Marc's happiness was then complete. Cynthia and Francis safe, Grigor and Niki Syeline secure in their new lives, the mission was a success. Carl, Phan Vihn and Kati Vogel had not forgotten to mention how Marc had shown extreme courage during those perilous hours. The congratulations that had been offered him gave him back all the self-confidence he so desperately needed.

His astrobus took off. When it touched down at the Elysee astroport, six hours later, he knew that Erymede was finally his true home.

Glossary

Crenel: a set of openings in the top of a wall or parapet.

Firth: a relatively narrow inlet of the sea.

Niello: a black compound of sulphur and silver, lead or copper used to cut a design onto a metal surface.

Parapet: a low wall or railing along the edge of a roof.

Portcullis: an iron or wooden grating suspended vertically in grooves in the gateway of a castle or fortified town and able to be lowered so as to bar the entrance.

Postern: a small rear door or gate in a rampart or castle.

Promontory: a high point of land, especially of rocky coast, that juts out into the sea.

Scorpion's Treasure
Translated by Frances Morgan

Luc and Benoit, teenage sons of farmers in the village of Neuborg near Quebec in 1647 New France, discover a mysterious cave. Then they witness the arrival by night of a mysterious ship and the unloading of heavy bags which the sailors take to the cave. A second visit to the cave confirms that it's a treasure.

How Luc and Benoit become involved with the captain who has left his treasure at Neuborg, and how their lives are endangered as a result make for an absorbing tale.

ISBN 0-88753-211-X $5.95

The Sword of Arhapal
Translated by Frances Morgan

In the small town of Neubourg near Quebec, the magical sword Arhapal is stolen.

Guillaume and Didier, two teenagers from Neuborg, begin investigating the theft. Didier gains access to the manor where the sword is hidden. His efforts to regain the sword, sometimes aided and sometimes threatened by unseen watchers, lead him into great danger. As he finds himself trapped in the cellars of the manor with a madman clutching the Sword Arhapal and rushing his way, it seems doubtful that he will survive.

ISBN 0-88753-212-8 $5.95

Beyond the Future

By Johanne Massé
Translated by Frances Morgan

Three astronauts, orbiting Earth aboard a space shuttle during World war 3, see their home world devastated by a nuclear holocaust. Their own ship is hurled into the future by the shock-waves; they land on a completely transformed Earth. How they survive, and the strange time-twist surrounding the life of one crew-member, makes for a fascinating science fiction fantasy adventure.

ISBN 0-88753-210-1 $5.95

Lost Time

By Charles Montpetit
Translated by Frances Morgan

While hiding in a closet, Marianne feels her brain being invaded by an entity capable only of time travel (whereas we humans are capable only of space travel). The entity soon leaves Marianne, but her body dies from the shock of the encounter. Her mind survives, though, in symbiosis with that of the entity, and she demands a new body to live in.

Their search through time begins: the girl finds herself in a host of bodies such as that of a nineteenth sentury teacher chased by murderous students. None of the attempts prove successful, and Marianne grows desperate to find a solution...

ISBN 0-88753-208-X $5.95

The Invisible Empire
By Denis Côté
Translated by David Homel

Nicholas is shocked by the murder of his musical idol after one of his pacifist meetings which Nicholas has attended. A series of clues soon puts Nicholas on the track of a conspiracy involving religious cults. By joining the Church of Balthazar he learns about a sinister cult whose leaders want to put an end to the liberal movement and social degeneration. Only when Nicholas is called upon to prove his loyalty to the cult by murdering a rock star, however, does he discover the full impact of the cult upon his life and family.

ISBN 0-88753-213-6 $5.95

Shooting For the Stars!
By Denis Côté
Translated by Jane Brierley

Michel Lenoir, hockey star, lives in luxury, and realises nothing of the social problems of his times (2010): the scarceness of food, water and natural resources, the wide scale unemployment, the poverty, the police repression.

Only when Michel is enlisted for a series of hockey matches against a team of robots does he begin to understand the collusion between his own manager and the robot industry, and the secret power of a caste of dehumanised old men who control the world economy.

ISBN 0-88753-215-2 $5.95